Diary of a Misplaced Philosopher

To Monika,

Happy birthday!   On this special
day of your life, I wish you
much happiness and all the best
for the future. Now you're 21 — gosh
that old, you'll have to ~~start~~ stop
arriving everywhere in a hurry panting
and sometimes late! Ha Ha Ha!
Have a splendid b'day (bidet) and
don't get too drunk or you won't
be able to tell your kiddies + grandkiddies
about your day etc..
Take care, and be happy!

Lots of love

Saul

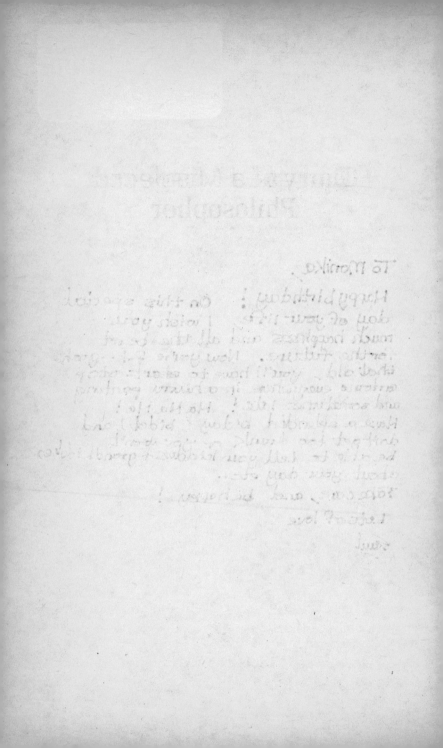

Diary of a Misplaced Philosopher

Joseph North

BLACK SWAN

All of the characters in this book are fictitious and any
resemblance to actual persons, living or dead, is
purely coincidental.

DIARY OF A MISPLACED PHILOSPHER

A BLACK SWAN BOOK 0 552 99403 0

Originally published in Great Britain
by Bloomsbury Publishing Ltd.

PRINTING HISTORY

Bloomsbury edition published 1989
Black Swan edition published 1990

This book is set in 11/12 pt Mallard
by Colset Private Ltd., Singapore.

Black Swan Books are published by
Transworld Publishers Ltd., 61–63
Uxbridge Road, Ealing, London W5 5SA, in
Australia by Transworld Publishers
(Australia) Pty. Ltd., 15–23 Helles Avenue,
Moorebank, NSW 2170, and in
New Zealand by Transworld Publishers
(N.Z.) Ltd., Cnr. Moselle and Waipareira
Avenues, Henderson, Auckland.

Made and printed in Great Britain by
Cox & Wyman Ltd., Reading, Berks.

Prudientiori credamus, stultiori remittamus

Seneca, *De Ira*

27 February

Denzil Rackman, who was at Oxford with me ten years ago, has since done better in life than I, and has recently bought a large Victorian house in Empire Road, Catford, paying off the mortgage by letting rooms to needy acquaintances. I moved in last month and am finding it a decreasingly desirable residence. Rackman is as moody as an adolescent girl, his latest pretext for a grumble being my frying some of Dalli's Merguez sausages. 'It's not so much the smell,' he moaned, 'but you're destroying the fabric of the house.' Clearly he is heading for a nervous breakdown. I pointed out that, throughout the annals of quantity surveying, there are no records of a house's having fallen down because sausages were fried in it, to which he retorted that the sausages gave off a greasy miasma which would eat into the paintwork of the bedrooms. Since the bedrooms are miles from the kitchen, and since in any case Rackman is intending to redecorate them in the autumn, this seemed a flimsy reason to stop a poor fellow from enjoying his sausages. He went on, perhaps by way of conciliation, 'This is the only bone of contention.' 'I'm glad you think so,' I replied, and he stalked off to do some nocturnal gardening, of which he is suspiciously fond. Often, as dusk falls, he is to be found digging in a large hole at the bottom of the garden; I am keeping my eyes open for bottles of Jeyes fluid about the house and, when I find one, shall inform the police.

Rackman occasionally goes parachuting. His last jump nearly ended in disaster: being corpulent, uninsured and about to land on a car, he had to take last-minute evasive action and landed on his bottom. As a result he has for the last few days been able to walk only by swinging his legs about in an odd way; it has been impossible to pass him on the stairs. He was recently given a medical checkup, his firm (he is an accountant) providing one for all its employees as they turn thirty, presumably to see whether it is worth their contributing to the pension fund. Rackman was told by the doctor – for reasons to do with his balls – to wear boxer shorts, and has since been sporting a pair with scenes from *The Flintstones* on them. He was also given a lifesize X-ray photo of his torso. Seeing a large lump in the middle, he was convinced he had a malign tumour, until the doctor explained that this was his heart.

On Wednesday I had some riff-raff to dinner, including my dear friend Simon Abram, science editor of *World Affairs Magazine*. Like many of my guests, he prefers me to conduct him to my Catford residence from Charing Cross, the middle class being daunted by journeys to areas of London unserved by the tube. At London Bridge we had to change and were embroiled in a M. Hulot situation, running backwards and forwards between platforms 1 and 4 to be greeted each time by an announcement that the train we had just risked heart-attacks to catch was cancelled 'due to' staff shortage, leaf on line, or something else. These ad hoc announcements are delivered with less elocutionary finesse than the standard recorded ones; the recordings were obviously made in the fifties or earlier by a nice lady with a *Brief Encounter* voice, who tells you that the train will stop at Bexleh and that you should mind the gep between train and pletform.

I am widely known as the Escoffier of Empire Road, for my dinners are elaborate affairs. The evening before,

I had bought a tin of Bolognese sauce, and I managed to persuade Abram to cook the spaghetti. A vegetarian who turned up was prevailed on to cook herself some broccoli, and another lady came with a small plastic bag containing slices of pork – but these were superfluous and I shall have them for lunch today. One trouble with living some miles from central London and having a local station at which one train in twenty stops (and those only between 8 a.m. and 9 a.m. on weekdays), is that one's *convives* tend to rush off as soon as they have inserted the last mouthful, and one is left alone with a pile of washing up and *The World Tonight* or *Music in Our Time* at 10.30 p.m. I have tried offering people a bed for the night, but the women think I am trying something on, as, often, I am. Abram made the excuse that he had to go home to put on a smart suit as he was going to an interview the following morning. It turned out, however, that he was giving it; he is looking for an assistant to help with the science page. Various young scientists have applied for the job, some of them with interesting specialities: one has just been researching into the levels of cortisone found in driving instructors' spittle.

7 March

I run the philosophy and social science department of Simpkin Scholarly Books (Literary Property and Libraries Bought), an emporium of academic cast-offs behind St Martin's Lane. On Monday I went to Manchester to see Dr Kropach, who had offered us a collection of 1,500 volumes of German sociology, just shipped from Argentina and doubtless the library of a Nazi war criminal with a new identity. Kropach, a historian, has a business in old books which he runs like the Scarlet Pimpernel. We first came across him when, at an auction, a colleague of mine thought he felt his pocket being picked, but found in fact that something had been put *into* it – a shred of paper saying, 'If you want to buy some important books, come to the Burger King at 11 o'clock'; the author of the note was Kropach. Whenever I have been to see him, he has asked me to meet him in a post office. This time he was late, so, in order not to look as if I were loitering with intent, I passed the time filling in a form for a Mobility Allowance. Then, after a lunch of (in my case) a dozen oysters – one of which had a kind of aquatic caterpillar crawling around it and another was of an ominous creamy consistency – Kropach drove me to a high-rise on the outskirts, parking in an underground carpark whose electronic portcullis closed behind us as we drove in. Pretending to be Sean Connery, I followed K into a lift which took us to a tiny flat full of books on the thirty-first floor. What K's reason is for embedding his transactions in a B-movie plot is unclear; perhaps he wants to avoid tax (this is suggested by the fact that he forbids us to write to him and sends us unsigned invoices), or perhaps he wants his life to have more colour than can be found in weekly lectures on agricultural developments in the early modern period. The full extent of his shadiness was revealed this time, the sociology books being in the last stages of decay, the semi-detached spines flapping to reveal strips of metal – presumably part of an unsuccessful theft prevention system.

On Tuesday evening I went to dinner chez Moses Nebith, my assistant and former fellow-student, a tiny philosopher of some brilliance and erudition with an impressive range of hates (Jonathan Miller being one of the more prominent ones: if you want to make little Moses go purple and roll on the floor, you need only say that J. Miller is a genius). He lives in Camberwell in a council flat reminiscent of *The Caretaker*, where he served me vegetable soup and chocolate digestive biscuits and played me tapes of a large number of members of the Bach family.

Everyone knows that JS Bach had several musical offspring, but little M, at age twelve, started a society for promoting the music of all the Bachs, including some of JS's ancestors. The other evening he played me a rather sombre piece by JS's great-uncle. He also unrolled a Bach family tree, and my eye was caught by someone called Lips Bach – a brass-player perhaps. Moses visits a shrink three times a week (a colleague observed that, judging by his size, the treatment seemed to have been successful). The couch in the consulting room is covered by one of those open-work blankets that look like aertex under a microscope. One day M had a biro in the back pocket of his trousers, which hooked on to the blanket, so, when he got up at the end of the session, he trailed the blanket out of the room behind him. The shrink said nothing, apparently thinking this was a revealing parapraxis. Little M only noticed his appendage when he got outside, so he left it hanging on the banisters.

14 March

One of the unacceptable faces of secondhand bookselling is the writing of death letters. When an obituary appears in *The Times* of someone who is likely to have had a large library, Simpkin sends to 'The Executors of Professor X Dec'd' a letter beginning 'We have hesitated to approach you' and carrying on about how, if they want to flog the old boy's books, we shall be able to offer them a decent price. The reason given for this claim in the letter is that the shop has connections with Japanese universities, who are prepared to pay a premium in order to buy, at one stroke, a whole collection made by someone – viz. the stiff – who knew what he was doing. I have always been uneasy about the force of this argument, since the older generation must contain plenty who have unhappy wartime memories of Japan, but we have never received an enraged reply. I am the executive responsible for ambulance- (or rather, hearse-) chasing, and am given free copies of *The Times* for the purpose (I only ever read the obits and the page saying what is on the radio). The sending of the letter is not irksome, for, while I am hesitating to approach the executors, little Moses is looking up their address, and, since the letter is already on the word processor, we only have to type in the address and a couple of occurrences of the deceased's name in order to produce a personalized message of insinuation. Visiting the libraries is more of a strain, for The Executors are invariably a lonely and grief-stricken old lady living on the outskirts of a university town in one room of a house that is now too big for her. When I, the Grim Reader, appear, the neighbours must shudder behind their net curtains, reflecting that soon one of the chilling missives will be dropped on their own doormat and all their books will be taken away. I have considered wearing a special black uniform for the visits and perhaps carrying a large scythe; I have also discussed with our proprietor the possibility of sending very frightening letters to very frail academics *before* their demise, in order to make trade more brisk – or looming up at their windows, dressed in a sheet. It would, however, be worth inducing heart-attacks only in the humanities; I soon gave up writing to dead scientists, as none of them has any books worth buying. Among the arts subjects history produces the best collections, though I suspect that the generation of historians who are now croaking is the last to have been able to afford large numbers of hardbacks. My latest catch, collected on Monday, was the library of the late Professor Goff of Oxford, a historian of the Byzantine era.

I returned to London in time to have dinner with Anita Bullock, another former fellow-student, who believes and retails the most preposterous stories and is therefore a good medium for spreading rumour. Some time ago I told her that a mutual acquaintance had a sister who was seven feet tall, and later had the same story told to me by someone further along the chain of credulity. Anita now writes reports for a management consultancy (several bankruptcies are expected shortly) run by Derek Badham, a friend of mine who, presumably with a view to offering me a job, had asked her to tell me what the work involved. Like ninty-nine per cent of those who have just completed a doctoral thesis in philosophy and for whom the obvious career is one in a university, I am wondering what to do next, there being no hope of a philosophy job in Britain as the number of posts in British philosophy departments has declined by twenty-five per cent in the last five years. The situation is better – though not much – in the United States, so I took out a subscription to a slim and infrequent journal published by the American Philosophical Association, called *Jobs for Philosophers* (a companion to the book of Belgian jokes). I have been applying for almost every job it mentions and have been turned down by places that ought to have been grovelling to have me, such as the Slippery Rock Mormon Agricultural College and the Oshkosh Federal Institute of Correction. All the letters of rejection – word processed and personalized like the Simpkin death letters – say that there were between 200 and 300 applicants for the post, but I am not confident of finding a job at the three hundredth attempt. American graduate students are in a stronger position, as their departments compile elaborate 'dossiers' to accompany their applications, while a British student is armed only with a c.v., a sample of written work and a couple of testimonials written with English understatement. Dan Hole – my tutor at the University of London, where I did my graduate work – said that for me to compete in the American philosophy job market is like a man with a tobacco plant in his front room competing with the manufacturers of Marlboro.

Undaunted, this Christmas I went to the APA annual convention in Boston, where several thousand actual and aspiring philosophers interview each other for jobs while pretending to attend seminars. True to Hole's forebodings, I failed to secure a single interview and wandered round the Boston Sheraton like a leper, reflecting that a well-placed bomb in the Grand Ballroom would vacate half the American philosophy jobs with one bang. I would have sulked in my hotel bedroom, but the room overlooked a building site and men with hard hats kept peering through the window. A fanatic, or a genius with a Copernican Revolution to effect, would continue philosophizing as an impoverished nonentity without a job; other qualified philosophers do better to abandon philosophy. Whether I shall become a management consultant is doubtful, since Anita seems to work like a slave for little more than I get tootling around in ye worlde of olde bokes (but then I only have Anita's word for it). The usual resorts of failed philosophers are computers and the law, and I shall probably go for the latter.

21 March

Enthusiasts for *Psycho* and *The Texas Chainsaw Massacre* will regret not having accompanied me to Kestleton, Yorks., to visit Miss Prudence Crispe, only daughter and sole executrix of the late Professor Crispe, an authority on Chinese religions. I had been told that Kestleton was in an Area of Outstanding Natural Beauty, so, when I got on to a little train at Leeds for the last stage of the journey, I was surprised to find myself rattling through an industrial wasteland of abandoned and crumbling Victorian factories and stopping at quaint little stations with such names as 'British Steel' and 'Cargo Terminal'. The other passengers consisted of a young woman with a child suffering from whooping cough, a man in a wheelchair whose embittered expression suggested resentment at inadequate compensation for an industrial accident and two skinheads (one with a black eye) who laughed at my trilby hat. It reminded me of the train Woody Allen gets on at the beginning of *Stardust Memories*.

At Kestleton Central I was met by Miss Crispe, a prattling, quivering *reductio ad absurdum* of demented spinsterhood with the wild eyes of an Irish wolfhound and a spine-chilling grin of grey teeth that flashed at moments unpredictable from the course of conversation (or, rather, monologue). On the phone I had proposed taking a taxi from the station, but she refused to hear of it, telling me in hushed tones, 'It costs £1.30, you know.' We drew up on an arterial road on the outskirts of the town, beside one of a row of bungalows dating from the thirties. Many people who live in insalubrious areas have bits of rubbish in their front garden, tossed in by passing louts, but Miss C had piles of it, not only in the front but all round the house. Either she suffers from prowlers or she throws it there herself. This was a mere foretaste of the Augean Stables indoors: all ten square feet of floorspace were strewn with knitting, laundry, empty biscuit packets and other waste. I shuddered to see, on the sitting-room table, the 'cold collation' she had promised me – a plate of antique Mr Kipling almond slices and some sandwiches, prepared some weeks previously, whose corners had curled up to reveal an unidentifiable form of pale meat (part of another visiting bookseller perhaps) – and, promising myself some Travellers-Fare from the Leeds station buffet at teatime, pretended that I was in too much of a hurry to eat. After Miss C had shown me into the matchbox of a room where her father had obviously been confined in his twilight years, in which he had died and in which his books had remained, I suggested that she might like to leave me to look through them. A look of horror crossed her face (how many books did she think I could squeeze into my

15

briefcase?). 'Oh no, I'd better stay,' she said, and sat two feet behind me on the old man's bed, knitting demonically. Fortunately I found reasons, other than panic at the thought of ever setting foot in Kestleton again, for not buying the collection.

Thence to North Bromsdyke Polytechnic, where I met the librarian, Mr Falk. North B's philosophy department is threatened with closure, so, reflecting that its members, soon to join me on the academic scrapheap, would no longer be using the library, I had planned – like the inmate of Belsen who tortures fellow-prisoners to gain favour – to relieve the library of all its philosophy books. Falk liked this idea but, being enslaved to institutional protocol, he suggested that, when the department does close, the best way for the books to be transferred from the polytechnic to Simpkin would be for him to give them to us and for us coincidentally to make an appropriate donation to the library fund, whose interest is untaxed.

I was next introduced to Dr Leech, head of the sociology department, who wanted to sell me all the books belonging to the former anthropology department, which the sociology dept. has now subsumed. (Further to the Government's policy of bringing all higher education in Britain to an end, sociology is itself to be swallowed by a third department next year.) Leech's motive was hatred of the one remaining anthropologist on the premises, whom he described as 'an obnoxious individual who never looks at the books anyway'. Unfortunately, just as I started looking at the books, the obnoxious individual – a Hungarian – came into the room and demanded to know who I was. When I said 'a bookseller', he flew into a rage about not having been consulted, and Leech only managed to hustle him into the corridor by means of some transparent casuistry to the effect that I had not come to the polytechnic in order to inspect the books but just happened to be looking at them while I was there on other business. Clearly, as the ship sinks, the rats have decided to murder each other.

28 March

On Tuesday evening little Moses and Louise (another colleague from Simpkin) came to dinner. I had also invited Moses' girlfriend Judy; she is a vegetarian, so I had planned a cheese fondue – another reason for the plan being that Rackman, who was also expected, frequently makes cheese fondues for parties and could therefore have been coaxed into preparing this one. But neither Judy nor Rackman appeared; the latter had to spend the evening in the RAC Club being upbraided for lack of commitment by some superiors in his firm, the former had been stricken by a disease of the stomach that prevented her from eating milk products. Although Moses and Judy have been living as man and wife for some years, it is unlikely that their relationship will ever be sanctioned by more than the common law, for M's father will disown him if he marries a goy. Nebith *père* is not, however, a rabbi but a minister of the Californian Universal Life Church – an office he bought by mail order for $20 and which entitles him to conduct marriage ceremonies in California. He is also a Kentucky colonel – the sort, like Colonel Sanders, who had never been near a body of armed men – and insists on being called 'colonel'.

In Rackman's absence I resorted to a cookery book which gave away its age, first, by calling the concept of a meal cooked at table 'one of the gayest entertaining ideas of recent years', and second, by displaying on its cover a lady – whom I failed to amuse my guests by trying to imitate – in a mini skirt and beehive hair-do. The fondue was a triumph, though the recipe's 'serves four' was a lie, and I would have enjoyed it more if my mother had not told me that cheese fondue is a lower-middle-class dish. Culinary snobbery is an area in which I am a novice; I once provoked gales of deriding laughter at a dinner chez Eugenia ffiske (another Simpkinienne) by revealing a preference for trifle. Eugenia would presumably have smiled with indulgent pity at the blackcurrant jelly I produced for the next course, though it was treated with the respect it deserved by Louise, a slim, silent, apologetic-looking woman of twenty-eight with a Habsburg chin and what was described, in a testimonial supporting her application for a job at Simpkin, as a 'fragile' sense of humour. For the past three years she had slid round the shop (her feet, perhaps because she wears shoes that are too large, never leave the ground, so if she approaches you from behind she can be detected by a shuffling noise) and now works as assistant to Maurice Montague, the manager, sharing a tiny office with him and one Fein. MM has a low voice, and Fein a high one; the three of them recall Bill and Ben and Little Weed. Your first impression of Louise is that she is a mouse but, once her fragile sense of humour has revealed itself in the knowing look she gives you as Maurice talks some nonsense or other, you decide there is more to her than meets the eye. She is a talented linguist, someone observing of her recently that she is the only employee at Simpkin who is able to be silent in three languages.

The following evening Franziska came to Empire Road to eat a sausage and be inspected by Rackman as a possible second tenant. She is a student from Berlin in her early twenties whom I met at a philosophy conference. Rackman was smitten, thus transferring his affections to a woman half his age from one twice his age. For the last few years he has been having intimate relations with a woman police constable – a lady of fifty-two with two grandchildren. Feeling that she was being exploited by R, the granny recently ditched him for her gynaecologist, who apparently drives a Rolls Royce; R observed bitterly that, with the gynaecologist, certain preliminaries would be circumvented. Though I am not anxious for the peace of the Empire Road Hermitage to be disturbed, Franziska would in some ways be an asset; during

18

the evening I learnt the German for 'glands' and 'jelly', and she endeared herself to me – though not to the landlord – by recounting how she had once let a kettle boil dry because she was engrossed in *Wallenstein*. She did not however seem to relish the prospect of life with two thirty-year-old buffers, preferring to remain in a bohemian council house in the groin of the Metropolitan line, i.e. at the point where the lines to New Cross and New Cross Gate diverge. Since the house is shaken constantly by trains passing on both sides, Rackman and I must be an even more rebarbative couple than we realized.

4 *April*

Not only am I a man with a Leibnizian range and depth of culture, I am also a prig who, like the author of the *Minima Moralia*, will find the work of the devil in apparently the most innocent avatar of mass culture. My mother, on the other hand, who was educated beyond her range of sensitivity, has spent the half-century since she left Oxford in an orgy of intellectual akrasia, reading thrillers, listening to the BBC Concert Orchestra, falling asleep in performances of Shakespeare and – the obsession of her life's autumn – tap dancing. Our tastes can often be reconciled – I will hum a passage from Mozart's piano concerto K414 and she, finding that it shares the same sequence of notes as the opening of 'Some Enchanted Evening', will then give a rendition of the latter (she can, in fact, find a dance-hall tune to coincide with any piece from the classical repertoire) – but they occasionally clash, as they did last Saturday evening when I wanted to listen to some Webern and she wanted to watch the unspeakable Parkinson interview Jack Lemmon and Walter Matthau on a programme called (absurdly in this instance) *One to One*. The Old Dear banged some cutlery around and I became sulky and menacing, but, being a kid fist in an iron glove, I capitulated; Parky was turned on, the OD immediately nodded off, and I was left watching by myself, knowing that, if I turned the idiot-box off and the record player on, she would wake up and accuse me of high-handedness. As it happened, Matthau made me fall about with merriment, so I was glad the OD was not awake.

On Monday I went to pick up a suit I have been having made. It is a rough tweed with turn-up trousers and makes me look like Dr Finlay. Being about to forsake the world of universities and secondhand books, I should never have ordered it, for no city lawyer was ever seen in such a thing, except at weekends. When my measurements had been taken at the shop, they were sent to the tailor, who returned them saying that they were unbelievable, and I had to be measured again. I could not bring myself to ask the assistant whether I in fact have an unbelievable shape or he had misrepresented me. Buying clothes is often humiliating. A while ago I went to buy a hat at Bates, which *prima facie* is an old-fashioned purveyor of headwear to gentlemen and *secunda facie* is a tourist trap. (My suspicions were aroused when I found in the shop a glass case containing a stuffed cat dressed like Mr Sponge and sporting a top hat suitable for the feline head.) Having seen in the window a rather louche wideawake which I thought would make me look like Lytton Strachey, I asked to try it on. 'You can't wear that,' the salesman barked, 'you've got a small face.' I insisted nevertheless and, when I had put it on, he stood me in front of the glass and sighed in a tired voice, 'The mirror never lies, sir.' While he was searching for something more suited to my tiny phiz, I asked, just to make conversation, what size my head was. 'Oh God,' he cried, rummaging through boxes and not looking at me, 'they all want to know what size their head is; every time, it comes out like a record, "What size is my head?" It doesn't *matter* what size your head is!' By this time I was becoming tearful, and almost fell on the neck of an old American lady sitting in the corner, who said, of the hat the dragon finally instructed me to buy, 'Thatsh vury becoming.'

Little Moses is now the most frequent visitor to the Empire Road Athenaeum. On Thursday I subjected him to another fondue. He is so depressed that he gets up at 11.00 a.m. and, unless he is out, watches telly all evening. To raise his spirits I gave him a pipette-full of vodka, which caused him to dance the Charleston and to start shouting about the transvaluation of all values. He expressed the intention of writing a book about sexual perversion and said he could not decide whether to make it theoretical or confessional. 'Confessional!' Rackman and I cried, hoping for some titbits. But even in his cups he kept his counsel.

11 April

On Wednesday, having announced at Simpkin that I was going to the dentist, I went to be interviewed as a prospective articled clerk by Mr Richard Horn of Savage Borman, a large firm of solicitors in the city. I was nervous about this, for I had met Horn a couple of months previously, having gone to see him to talk in general terms about the possibility of my becoming a lawyer. On that occasion, when I was shown into his office, he was standing, looking away from the door and out of the window; obviously knowing that I had entered, he continued to stare out of the window in order to make me squirm. When eventually he swung round, it was with a menacing leer and the words, 'Mr Wilkinson!' 'No, North.' A pause, the leer frozen on his face. 'From Milton Keynes?' 'No, Catford.' The leer is replaced by an expression of rage; Horn bolts to his telephone and hammers the buttons like Liszt playing a fortissimo. Failing to get a reply within two seconds, he bangs the receiver down and rushes from the room shouting, 'You've completely thrown me!' On the second occasion, however, he was in his Dr Jekyll phase and we had a pleasant conversation about Catford and Oxford, in which he had been respectively brought up and educated. My prospects of being taken on by Savage B are, I think, good, which is a relief, as the pleasures of selling formerly enjoyed books are dwindling. I returned to Simpkin to witness a heated debate between Maurice and Fein about the date of the first appearance in print of *Auld Lang Syne*, a topic almost as gripping as another recently raised by Fein, namely the date of the invention of the pencil sharpener. Fein claimed that the first pencil sharpener was horse-drawn, but I find the instrument hard to imagine. I assume that the hole faced upwards, so that the pencil stood vertically, and that a string attached the pencil to the horse, which (like the mules used to pump water in primitive places) walked in a circle, thereby rotating the pencil in the sharpener.

Lost property. Anyone who found, on the 17.59 Charing Cross–Gravesend service last Thursday, a Simpkin carrier bag containing:

  (i) three tupperware boxes with Wall's icecream labels
 (ii) a pair of galoshes
(iii) a kipper

should return it please to 12 Empire Road SE6. The boxes were given me by Old Simpkin, my employer, who said they would be useful for keeping houmus in (given their size, he must be accustomed to feeding houmus to Greek elephants); the galoshes are essential attire for anyone still wearing his father's shoes in the tenth April after his father's death; the kipper may be kept as a reward by the finder. Rackman, noting my dejection, kindly produced a kipper the following day, though I don't think it was the one that went to Gravesend. He also fed me handsomely when his brother and his brother's boyfriend came to dinner. Rackman *frère* is at least as large as my landlord and began the evening by asking the latter what he now weighed; evidently they are competing for the title of this year's Tichborne Claimant. He looked alarmed when my Rackman told him that he had just had a second ECG test, which he described as humiliating because it involved his chest's being shaved. If I had been given such a test, I should have been more humiliated by the fact that it would have been unnecessary to shave mine.

18 April

The best event of the week was the arrival of a letter from Savage Borman offering me articles and promising to pay the fees for training as a solicitor. The worst event of the week was meeting Leslie. The elderly WPC, doubtless feeling bitter about the ending of her affair with Rackman (v.28 March) and wanting to play him a dirty trick, recommended Leslie as a second lodger, and on Tuesday evening he came to inspect the Empire Road Palazzo. A tubby, bald little chap, he reminded me of Peter Glaze. Despite having been advertised as quiet, he babbled with fatuous and obtrusive geniality about the South Circular Road and a diversion at Nunhead and, being an accountant (an unqualified one), he soon engaged Rackman in a merry and opaque conversation couched wholly in initials and acronyms. Having glared at him in silence for a few minutes, I went to sulk over the *Times Higher Education Supplement*, which Leslie took to be *The Sporting Life*. 'Doing the gee-gees?' he asked jovially. This is the man whose pubic hairs will from now on fill the plughole, whose warmth will be felt on the lavatory seat and whose grinning face will be popping round the door of my study with a 'Mind if I join you?'

Neville Frost and his girlfriend Sara came to dinner on Thursday. He was at school with me; as with Blafaphas and Fleurissoire in *Les Caves du Vatican*, his facial hair in adolescence was as lush as my acne. In fact, in the space of one Easter vacation, he turned from a little angel with a fluty voice into a swarthy Levantine, which he has remained ever since; when he went up to Cambridge he had trouble convincing the librarian that he should have an undergraduate's ticket and not a visiting scholar's. We are in many ways physically complementary: although we are approximately the same height, my legs are twice as long as his, so that, when we are sitting next to each other, he looms over me but can barely touch the floor with his toes. He is now an actor, for which he is quite unfitted by his considerable, but now festering, intellect. At university there were plenty of mature roles for which his appearance suited him, but in the real world there are plenty of really mature people to play them, so he does not do very well.

25 April

My mother has a country seat called Frogs Cottage in Goose End, Suffolk, where we both usually go for weekends. Having a hair appointment in the local town with Gino of Italy, the Old Dear had gone up early, so I was forced to travel on a Lightning Omnibus – a mobile inferno of extreme heat, migraine, screaming and mismanaged infants, youths with audible walkpersons, giggling girls and stupid old women clacking their outrageously uniform dentures and dropping boiled sweets which then rolled around the floor. I tried to pretend I was Marcus Aurelius. In the shed at the cottage I found a little trolley for distributing powders on lawns and,

24

like a toddler, pushed it up and down, sprinkling – as I thought – moss eradicator. In fact all but one of the holes in the trolley's bottom were blocked, so only thin strips of the grass were treated; I discovered this when black tramlines started to appear on the lawn. Perhaps it is as well that most of the surface area are spared, for, since most of the lawn consists of moss, a successful application would have resulted in lawn eradication.

The OD had invited some people for dinner on Saturday including Clarence and Peggy Butt and Edie Fawcett. I have had a grudge against C. Butt since he called me impertinent eight years ago. The other night he demonstrated that old does not entail wise by saying that philosophy is about life and that, since we all part of life, philosophy should be comprehensible to everyone. You might as well argue that, since we all belong to the physical world, everyone should understand physics. Edie, who is eighty-two, was business manager in my father's office – which, according to my mother, explains why we are so poor – and used to share Frogs Cottage, paying a third of the bills. When she retired, she made it her sole residence, but my mother – who, soured by female rivalry, had hated her for years – announced to my father something like, 'Either that woman goes or I do', and we booted Edie out. She now lives, in a state of extreme senility, in a pleasant custom-built bungalow next door. Altzheimer has such a tight grip on her brain – particularly its linguistic centre – that it is often hard to tell whether she can't find the words for her ideas or hasn't any ideas either. It is just possible, by waiving the standard conversational rules against blatant self-contradiction, immediate repetition and non-sequitur, to talk with her *à deux*. But in company she lapses into silence, and on Saturday she concentrated on stuffing her fragile frame with food and drink sufficient for the army of Attila. Her gargantuan appetite is explained by the fact that she eats nothing at home, being too gaga to cook for herself and too proud (and, having in earlier days worked for the WRVS, probably too knowledgeable) to eat meals on wheels. Even in her prime she was not much of a cook, having always scholastically followed the instructions of recipe books in the face of glaring evidence of inedibility. Thus she once tried to persuade us to eat an obviously raw steak and kidney pie (as it was brought to the table, my mother said 'Oh Christ' in a loud voice) by telling us that it had been in the oven for the time specified by Philip Harben; but perhaps she had not turned the oven on. Conceding finally that to eat it as it stood would result in certain botulism, she removed the bits of kidney and threw in some hard-boiled eggs.

As Edie's mind lapses into ever deeper darkness, her neighbours keep an increasingly close eye on her. My mother, catching her about to drive off to the shops on Easter Monday, pointed out that nothing would be open. 'Yes,' Edie replied, 'but the shops will be nice and empty this soon after Christmas.' It is doubtful that she should be driving at all; Mr Bird – a widowed and retired man from the Pru, who is our neighbour on the right (Edie, living on our left, has been christened 'the Loony Left' by mamma) – has more than once had to rescue her when she has run out of petrol, for she never looks at the gauge. Once she drove into a garage and said grandly, 'Fill her up!' 'That will be ten pence, madam,' the attendant said, returning after a few seconds. Her grasp of technical matters is generally rather frail. When she complained that there was nothing but news on the radio, my mother pointed out that she didn't have to listen to Radio 4, 'There are plenty of other programmes, Edie; you can listen to whatever you like.' Edie stared at her in amazement and then, pointing towards the sky, said, 'But how do they know what I want to hear?'

A threatening situation arose yesterday at Simpkin. Geoffrey Denley, an elderly homosexual employee with many rough trade connections, came out of the heraldry and military department in a state and told Eugenia that he had in there a man who used to work for Simpkin and who had been locked up for many years after having attempted to castrate his own father. After a hair-raising account of the number of barred doors one had to go through when visiting this Oedipus in the nick, Geoffrey said, 'He's all right now, so long as you don't cross him.' Eugenia, characteristically, spread the word, and soon every member of the firm had found a pretext for peering into heraldry and military. Maurice later met Geoffrey on the stairs, and said, 'What's this about a man who castrated his father?' – having failed to notice that Geoffrey's guest was standing just behind him. The result is not recorded, but I wouldn't like to be wearing Maurice's balls. 'I wouldn't like you to be wearing them either,' replied Maurice when I said this to him.

16 May

Pleasures are hard for the atrabilious chronicler to describe, so the following account of my holiday in Greece will be short. For five years I had had an apparently unrequited crush on Miss Rebecca Bochvar, and was therefore taken aback when she proposed that I drive her round the Peloponnese for two weeks. We flew – in a plane whose name, emblazoned on the fuselage in Greek letters, I suggested was the Attic translation of *Herald of Free Enterprise* (Miss B reprimanded me for tastelessness) – to Athens and, after eating the first two of a transfinite number of kebabs, wandered round the Plaka, which is like Carnaby Street with an acropolis. Having discovered that my companion snored at a volume likely to give Jack Ashley a start, I arose from a night of insomnia and insect bites and, squeezing with as much dignity as we could manage

27

into a Mini Metro, we set off through driving rain to Corinth. Lacking visual imagination and historical sense, I tend to be nonplussed by excavations, but Miss Bochvar recreated the glory that was ancient Greece by reading aloud, in her bell-like voice, choice passages from the *Blue Guide*, which, although written in the sixties, has the idiom of one hundred years earlier, saying for instance, of certain bits of rubble, that their significance is 'perceptible only to the antiquary'. By way of contrast, she had also brought *The Rough Guide to Greece*, which is dedicated to a nuclear-free Aegean and has a section on Feminismos, as well as a useful list of phrases such as 'Stop it' and 'I want to get off'.

We arrived in the evening at Mycenae, where we stayed in the same hotel as Schliemann and sat shivering in the restaurant – I wearing all three of the vests I had thrown, after swimming trunks and shorts, into my case (I wore all the vests on most days of the fortnight, rotating them for reasons of personal freshness), R wrapped in a blanket reading a copy of *Vogue* which for some obscure reason she had bought. Seeing my copy of *Moll Flanders* she remarked, 'How nice to have *Moll Flanders* and *Daniel Defoe* in the same volume!' The following morning we visited the Mycenaean ruins in a storm-force wind and then drove to the theatre of Epidauros, where we watched a team of Bulgarian cyclists – dressed in luminous anoraks and skin-tight satinette trousers – test its acoustics by dropping coins and rustling bits of paper. After Epidauros, Mistra, where my companion had a snore in the sun and we walked in the hills, sniffing the herbs, confessing that we didn't know the names of any of the plants, and going 'Aah' at herds of goats. Sparta now being notable only for the fact that the occupant of its postcard booth speaks Australian English, we drove on to Monembasia – where we disregarded the strains of 'A Whiter Shade of Pale' wafting from one of the Byzantine buildings that had been converted into a café – and then to Areopolis, gateway to the wild and rugged Mani, where feuding peasants used to throw things at each other from the tops of towers. Our days in the Mani were the most pleasant of the tour: the sun shone, Miss Bochvar displayed her corporeal magnificence by swimming naked, she sang (more than once) 'We're in the Mani', and we walked to Cape Tainaron, the supposed site of Hades.

One evening, as we were sipping our ninth ouzo, a Greek masher, with what P. Leigh-Fermor would describe as a 'rebellious' moustache, sat down at the next table, stared fixedly at Bochvar and started whistling and humming snatches of crooning melodies. Ignoring me, he offered her a cigarette, introduced himself as Dimitri and announced that he was a boatman in a cave full of stalactites (or so we inferred by radical interpretation from the exiguous linguistic data). At this point his wallet was produced, which contained a picture of himself in paratrooper's uniform and with a cigarette in his mouth which, he seemed to claim, he had been smoking while dropping 2,000 feet. My companion was looking profoundly impressed; so Dimitri, now in his stride, offered her a flower, saying, 'Because you are like a flower.' When he announced that he played the bazouki, I started fearing a nocturnal serenade and suggested that we eat our dinner elsewhere.

The second half of the holiday involved more motoring, which was a strain for the chauffeur, for, Greek roads containing axle-breaking potholes every fifty yards, a driver has to glue his eyes to the road surface while his passenger gazes at the scenery. Being incompetent, I usually managed to drive into the holes I swerved to avoid, and came to understand the note on the car-hire firm's contract which read, 'The company is not responsible for damage caused on roads without Aspait.' Moreover the Greeks clearly deserve their second place in the European league of car accident statistics – though most of the accidents seem to involve dogs; in the course of the tour we saw about thirty dead beside the road. I also had to right a tortoise that was lying on its back in the middle of a road, waving its legs about; when I did so, it hissed.

We oscillated, it seemed, between Butlin's holiday camps and places that appeared to have been untouched since the stone age; Delphi was submerged by coach parties while the people of Andritsena did not know what a tourist was. When we asked a local where the hotel was, he did an imitation of a man asleep, meaning that it had closed down because the patron had died. The old couple who ran the taverna, and obviously averaged three customers a year, pleaded with us to eat there. When, after looking into their pots, I hesitated, Miss B told me I was a 'Common Market prick', so, fearing she might run back to Dimitri, I capitulated and we ate the best meal of the holiday. Another memorable meal was had on our last night, in Vilya (which the *Blue Guide* identifies only as a chicken-farming centre), where we ate in a taverna that doubled as a butcher's – the owner hacking bits of meat off carcasses as they were ordered. The only part of the process that was not carried out in front of the customer was the slaughtering.

We flew home on a plane in which some seats had been removed to make room for a stretcher carrying an old lady with a drip attached to her arm. She looked as if she were going to see Heathrow and die, and during the flight a stewardess asked, 'Is there a doctor on board?' The oral examination for my Ph.D. was to take place four days later, so I thought optimistically of stepping forward. For the content and result of that examination, the reader is referred to the next instalment.

22 May

There are three possible outcomes to a Ph.D. examination: you can pass; you can fail (perhaps being given a derisory degree, like an M.Litt., for effort); or – worst of all possible worlds – your thesis can be 'referred', i.e. you are told to submit it again after rewriting bits. In philosophy – unlike the natural sciences, where you can pick up a doctorate for having cleaned your professor's test-tubes – failures and referrals are common, so, when I set off for the oral examination on my thesis *Set-Theory and the Paradox of the Heap*, I was uneasy – the more so since none of my teachers had been encouraging, one of them telling me, 'No-one has written philosophy like this since the Middle Ages.' He was referring to my tendency to spin discussions out into objections, replies, objections to replies, fivefold distinctions regarding replies to objections to replies, and so on; and advised me to register with a Catholic university, where, he said, scholasticism would be smiled upon. I was in fact worried that the thesis had made a dialectical mountain out of an ant's dropping, for I had recently written a paper to present the main results, and the paper, although one tenth as long as the thesis, seemed to leave nothing out.

The examiners were two ladies: Dr Weisberg, of the University of London, and Professor Fale, of the University of Newcastle. Four months had elapsed between my handing in my masterpiece and their getting in touch with me; while, during that time, my intellect was running to seed and I was forgetting everything I had written, it occurred to me that I had probably bored them to death and that they were sitting, slumped and undiscovered, over their respective copies. A kind friend suggested that the delay was probably to be explained by their having set going the procedure for awarding me a Nobel Prize. On the day, we met in Weisberg's room. My saturnine tutor Dan Hole was present 'to see that justice was done' but, in accordance with the rules, was not allowed to speak unless spoken to. He violated this restriction once, but was ignored. The examination was no piece of cake: Weisberg, who could have run rings round Socrates, opened proceedings with an objection, to which I had no answer, showing that what I had taken to be the most important chapter was redundant, and then, as I writhed, stammered and sweated, she and the prof batted me about, each one seizing on the answer I had just given to her fellow-torturer and turning it against something I had written in the thesis. After an hour and a half I asked, 'Does the procedure permit the examinee to pee?', which made them laugh, and, promising not to do any revision while I was out of the room, I tottered off in the hope of finding some untapped reserves of ingenuity, stamina or, at least, stoic virtue. When I returned they told me they had decided that we had talked long enough, and sent me out of the room again while they reached their verdict. I was re-admitted to be congratulated on having become Dr North, and I told them that I looked forward to forty years as an unemployed philosopher. So ended the philosophical period of my life: twelve years of Angst, exhaustion, hysteria and occasional exhilaration may be counted to have issued in success, since I now have an academic title and three published papers. The following morning I received a letter of acceptance from the National Institute of Professional Legal Studies (NIPLES), where I shall start this autumn. I had thought that by becoming a doctor I should stop being a figure of fun, but people now come up to me, say 'Dr North', and walk away laughing. Abram, a former philosopher turned lounge lizard, did not seem over-impressed. But this may be sour grapes due to his having only a 2.2 in the subject.

On Monday and Tuesday I was in Paris buying books with Stitt. Stitt is nominally my sidekick, and his ambition – now almost realized – is to reverse our roles. Since, while writing my thesis, I worked only part-time at Simpkin, Stitt's imperialist ambitions had free rein, and he now effectively runs the department. This is only the first step of his plan for world domination; running around the shop, he reads everyone's mail and insinuates himself into every conversation, thus knowing everything and being in a position always to bring the boss good news – for which, by the Cleopatra principle, he is then considered responsible – and to distance himself from disasters. I suggested to Stitt that he might like a battery of television monitors on his desk so that he could keep track of everything without having to run around, and pointed out that the screens could be attached to X-ray cameras so that he could read other people's letters before they open them. S smiled faintly at this expression of enraged impotence. When Old Simpkin asked me how Stitt and I were getting on, I could not resist making reference to his brazen pushiness, and Simpkin sought to console me by saying that the shop's personnel covered a spectrum ranging from scholars to hustlers. This was small comfort, for he added that the hustlers got paid more.

During the trip to Paris we had lunch with Joel Vuillard, a mathematician who dabbles in bookselling (a scholar *and* a hustler), and I sought to put Stitt in his place by asking V about the application of the Kuhnian model to the exact sciences. But V drinks so much and speaks so fast that his French is incomprehensible to all but the expert Francophone, so Stitt (an expert Francophone) soon managed to exclude me from the conversation and to turn it to current book prices. I was relieved at least that we were not eating in Vuillard's flat; on a previous visit I went to a party there and he served two varieties of fish yoghurt, one or both of which caused me a sleepless night. In fact I started feeling ill while still at the party, and, going to the lavatory, was surprised to find trigonometrical tables pinned to the door, presumably to allow V to refresh his memory while at stool. One would have thought that a professor at the Sorbonne would either know his tables or think that he was too grand to need to know them. The party was also memorable for the presence of two psychoanalysts, one of whom gave a rendition of a large part of *Carmen*, singing the various parts in different registers. Presumably this is a way of letting off steam after a day listening to people telling you why they want to fuck footwear. The other shrink was appropriately called Calligaris; he gave me a book he had written called *Hypothèse sur le phantasme*, which advances the thesis that we all have an unconscious desire to copulate with a 'monstrous body' (many people have realized this wish). I have been to Calligaris's flat, where I saw his cabinet and his cat, which had whiskers growing out of only one side of its face. Presumably to put me at my ease, he (Calligaris) took me to a restaurant called 'Aux Philosophes', where one could have a *salade Platon*, a *pâté Hegel*, and so forth. The connections between the dishes and their eponyms were opaque, though at least there were no *haricots Pythagore*. I avoided the *coupe Socrate* to be on the safe side.

30 May

Last weekend Rackman and I drove to Llandwynant in mid Wales to stay with Jeremy Hawthorn, a mutual friend from Oxford who has a cottage there. We took Franziska with us. (Or 'Transistor', as my mother misheard her name. The Old Dear is getting rather deaf. Recently she told me that *Minder* was back on the television. 'New series?' I asked. 'Of course I'm serious,' she replied.) It usually takes about four hours to get there, but on the pre-Bank Holiday Friday, to Rackman's fury, it took us ten and a half. There were various reasons for this. First, just before we set off, R noticed a bulge in one of his tyres, so we drove to a garage to have it inspected. 'Nothing to worry about,' said an elderly man with a badge saying 'Apprentice' on his pocket. But R, a cautious type, went for a second opinion to the Euro Exhaust Centre. 'Totally lethal,' the foreman there said, leaving me to wonder what partial lethality might be as we stood in the rain watching him operate a wonderful battery of machines to change the tyre. Having thus been delayed an hour or so, we got stuck for another two on the M1 and, when R had played through all his dreadful cassettes on the in-car entertainment system, we struck off across country to become hopelessly lost in (I think) Bletchley, where we ended up on a housing estate in a street called Whalley Drive. Our meandering crawl through merrie Englande brought us at nightfall to Worcester, where R evinced a sixth sense – or a refined sense of smell – in detecting, from no clues available to me, the location of the Indian restaurant. Here we were delayed several more hours, as R ploughed through a pile of Bombay duck and a plate of Biryani fit for a mammoth. The curry and the strain were too much for his chauffeuring powers, so he asked me to share the driving. This will make it harder for him to claim, next time I want to go to Tesco and ask to borrow his car (a company perk with rally wheels, gold metallic paint and a sloping back), that it is insured only for him to drive.

We arrived in Llandwynant at 1.30 a.m. and went straight to bed, though, in my case, not to sleep. To guarantee Transistor's privacy, I had to share a double bed with Rackman, who, spreading his fifteen stone over seven eighths of the surface area, started to emit a medley of loud noises, of which snoring was but one recurring motif; it was like sharing a bed with an industrial estate. I lay, clinging to the only available edge of the mattress, grinding my teeth and whimpering 'Oh God' until dawn had broken and the birds had started singing, and then tottered through the rain in my nightshirt to the car, where I found a sleeping bag, which I put on the stone floor of the kitchen and slept in feverishly

35

for the three hours before the other members of the party appeared for breakfast.

Our host arose first, an ebullient and charming *fainéant*, wholly lacking in malice, who seems to think of himself as a writer (the cottage contains several portraits of his two heroes – Lawrence and the man he calls 'Dullan Thomas'), but spends more time indulging in what he takes to be the necessary condition of creativity, viz. self-destruction through drink. He and Rackman were easily amusable; on two occasions I caused them to spit out food in mirth – the first time, in a self-styled 'Family Restaurant' in Aberdovey, where bits of Hawthorn's beefburger landed in my hair and behind my glasses. The weekend was an idyll of walking (H and R wheezing a hundred yards behind Transistor and my athletic self, their faces purple and their temples visibly throbbing), reading and hypaethral eating. During one of our meals on the terrace, as we watched the sheep eat Hawthorn's shrubs, it occurred to me that I would later look back on that moment with nostalgia, from which I inferred that I was happy.

Leslie is now installed in the Empire Road Exhaust Centre and is realizing my worst fears. The only comfort is that his life is coextensive with his work, so that he leaves the house at 6.30 a.m. and, if I bolt my dinner as soon as I arrive home from Simpkin, does not usually return till I have locked myself in my study for the evening. On Tuesday, however, he threatened my erotic prospects by hovering around while I was entertaining Miss Bochvar, who observed of him, when there was no reason to think he was out of earshot, 'I thought one only saw people like that on trains; I've always wondered where they lived.' In a recurrence of the sausage incident (v. 27 February) Leslie sided with me, pointing out to Rackman (the only smoker in the house) that cigarette smoke is at least as damaging as sausage steam to paintwork. Each of the three of us plays each of the other two off against the other, if you get my drift, and, after R had gone off to pursue his dark secret in the garden, L stayed with me in the kitchen to gossip about him. L sought to enlist me as a fellow plain man who would scoff with him at R's airy-fairy intellectual pretentions. 'He was talking to Franziska about Goethe!' he jeered. 'Cor!' I hooted weakly. Leslie has a chip on his shoulder, rightly, about not having been to one of the ancient universities, and complained that, when he writes reports, he is unable to match the elaborate prose of his Oxbridge colleagues. But, to vindicate his use of Morse code, he then asserted, as a matter of irrefragable scientific fact, that it is impossible for anyone to take in a sentence more than six words long. 'Surely not,' I answered, making sure I kept within the word limit, but did not think it worth supplying him with counterexamples. He compensates for his low intellectual station by snobbery about other things. When I asked him how his search for a house of his own was going (a subject close to my heart), he said he could not think of buying one in Catford because of all the 'coloureds'. Of course, this version of what he said has more than six words; I suppose he must have said something like 'Clearing off, Coloureds.'

6 June

Filial loyalty obliged me to go to Goose End last weekend to help the Old Dear entertain an even Older Dear – Mrs Adeline Keefe, aged ninety-two. Leaving aside the predictably horrific bus journey (this time I was sitting next to a mad woman who gabbled to herself from King's Cross to Chelmsford, occasionally breaking into demonic laughter; being in the window seat, I could only have escaped by climbing over her, which I was too frightened to do), duty was rewarded, for Adeline was an admirable vindication of old age, being lively, amusing and – a rare quality among the over-seventies – a firm believer in the external world. Edie was a sad contrast as she sat on the terrace, gawping at the guest (ten years older than she) whose merry conversation she was unable to follow. It is not just true that I want to be like Adeline when I am ninety-two; I want to be like her *now*.

For the last three years A has lent me, at a derisory rent, her house in Tuscany, where I have taken assorted *canaille*. It seems to be a place to take a partner you want to get rid of. The first holiday saw the collapse of a six-year relationship between Abram and a brash woman called Libby, who worked for breakfast television and might have stepped out of *The Ploughman's Lunch*; Abram, who had failed to notice how hard it was for his other friends to put up with her, was mortified by their congratulations. Shortly after the second holiday Mary Bruce left her husband, my dear Scottish friend Hamish; a keen observer might have inferred that something was up from the fact that she signed the house's visitors' book with her maiden name. The last holiday, however, marked the *beginning* of an affair, albeit an ambiguous and unhappy one. Dr Diana Radcliffe, of King's College, Cambridge, found irresistible the thought of a week watching Abram lying in his swimming trunks motionless except for the gentle waving of one big toe in time to the Mahler symphony coming through his Walkman, and pursued him to Tuscany. She was a medieval historian specializing in relics (hence her interest in Abram) and, whenever we visited churches, would drag us into the obscurest chapel and deliver a lecture about the bone standing in a jar on a shelf in the corner. The good doctor soon noticed that to the unprejudiced eye I was considerably more attractive than the toe-waving lizard, and she started gazing sultrily in two directions. On more than one evening, over dinner, A and I would each be stroking a different thigh of hers under the table. But it was pointless my competing with the Casanova of Cricklewood, and on our return to

England I left them to it. The affair ended with a bang when she accused him, rightly, of lack of commitment. Dr Radcliffe has since abandoned the academic life to become a hack journalist, applying her formidable erudition to the writing of fatuous articles about objets d'art and – *comble de malheur* – auctions of old books. This is surely at least as bad as *selling* old books, which she denounced on the holiday as a waste of time. On her change of career she displayed the naïve enthusiasm of a deb at her coming-out party, seeing herself as stepping through the college gates into the Real World where people earn lots of money, go to endless dinner parties and have fun, fun, fun.

This year I have been unable to get a group together, which may be as well, for the house's seclusion is now threatened on two fronts. Across the lane a hitherto empty house owned by one Signora Api (whenever she was mentioned, Abram would start singing 'Am so Api') now has tenants, and a heap of rubble behind Adeline's house has been turned into a holiday home by a friend of hers dubbed 'Squiffy' by members of my last party but one. The reason for the nickname is this. One day while we were there, he turned up to see whether he wanted to buy the rubble. He asked whether he could stay the night, producing (a) a letter of recommendation from Adeline and (b) six cans of beer. 'I brought beer,' he said, 'because wine makes me squiffy. I'm an alcoholic, you see, or rather, I'd *like* to be one.' None of us understood this. He then drank his way through the beer, and while dinner was being prepared had a few whiskies. When the first course appeared, he cried 'This looks marvellous!' and decided that he would join us in some wine after all. He drank more and more, exclaiming 'This looks marvellous!' whenever something was passed to him or brought to the table. The best thing to do when you are too drunk to speak is shut up, but Squiffy became more and more garrulous, trying to explain each slurred observation with an equally slurred meta-observation, and so on (literally) *ad nauseam*. By the time he launched – to our dismay – into a stream of semi-consciousness on the nature of philosophy, he had degenerated into spoonerisms, pronouncing 'moral' as 'Rommel'. At the end of the meal we piled the dirty dishes on the kitchen table. 'This looks marvellous!' leered Squiffy, catching sight of them as he lurched off to bed.

On Monday evening Rackman and I went to dinner at Mary's house. Both of us had eaten a large lunch of red meat, for Mary, a violinist in one of the London orchestras, is a veggie with culinary whims. As we waited for her to open the door, R for some reason stuck his fingers through the letter box. A terrible baying and howling resulted, for M is looking after two large dogs with a combined age of twenty-six, one of them epileptic, the other suffering from a character disorder. They belong to her sister, a woman in her mid-thirties who is on honeymoon with her seventy-six-year-old husband. Both sisters have odd ideas about wedlock, M having been undeterred from marrying Hamish by the fact that he gets up in the middle of the night to eat whole bulbs of garlic. When in happier days I asked M how she could bear to live with a man with such foul breath, she replied, 'I don't mind the garlic; it's just his eating anchovies in bed that I object to.' Since M and H split up, they have been closer than ever, visiting each other constantly and talking for hours on the phone.

This arrangement is perhaps preferable to a conventional marriage, with its appalling pressure of intimacy. I spent the following evening with a couple who could enrage each other by the most innocent actions, as when she helped herself to a bit of his taramasolata or he picked up her chequecard. We went to see *Tenue de soirée*, a faintly amusing bit of drivel about bisexuality. It was striking how much funnier the film seemed to be to the women in the audience than to the men, though this is perhaps explained by the fact that many of the former were French and could hence understand the dialogue, which was more amusing than the subtitles. When I was in Paris I went to a Marx Brothers film and rolled around in mirth, while the rest of the audience remained stony-faced; the subtitles were as funny as *The Dark Night of the Soul*.

On Wednesday I went to Cricklewood to have dinner with Abram and his father Solly. Abram *mère*, who married Solly when they were both very young, decided about ten years ago to have her adolescence before it was too late, and moved out, leaving father and son to get on with it. They live in a crumbling semi-detached house with stained bath and overgrown garden. Abram *fils* constantly increasing his *Lebensraum* by spreading his unread books over more and more of the available space. Solly is now squashed into one corner of the sitting-room with his telly and newspaper. They live on food from Marks and Spencer and served me cook-in-the-bag boeuf Stroganoff. Solly escaped from Austria in the war, and his English – like that of the Indians – is peppered with idioms of a bygone age; 'By Yove!' he will exclaim. He is a practising solipsist, and over dinner delivered a soliloquy about how careful one has to be when choosing a doctor. After dinner the younger Abram took me up to his room to listen to some records. He asked me – in the way one connoisseur might ask another whether he had heard a hitherto undiscovered motet by Okeghem – whether I knew Mendelssohn's Italian Symphony and, having put it on, fell asleep, leaving me to eat my way through his tin of biscuits. I learned one interesting fact during the evening. Abram *grandpère* had for many years a budgerigar which lived in a cage on the fridge. One day the fridge broke down, and the budgie died the day after.

I had promised to go on Thursday evening with Transistor to a concert, but, having by now tired of the gay round, I stood her up, feeling guilty, as she had – to

Rackman's jealous fury – brought a bouquet to me at Simpkin a few days before. The bouquet had clearly been picked from the embankment of the Metropolitan line at New Cross and looked like the kind of posy that peasants stick behind the ears of their mules, but I was touched none the less. I spent a quiet evening with Leslie; Rackman being away, we enjoyed an orgy of sausage frying with the windows shut.

12 June

Transistor, who clearly now thinks of Rackman and me as two old people who need meals on wheels, came to the Empire Road Nursing Home on Monday to cook dinner. She brought Jurgen, a huge former lover of hers from Berlin who was visiting for a couple of days. I had first met him at last year's International Wittgenstein Symposium in Kirchberg. On first acquaintance he seemed an intelligent and agreeable lad, so I invited him to accompany me to Vienna, where I was going to have a break from the Wittgenstein loonies. The first five minutes' conversation on the Kirchberg–Vienna train revealed him to be a pompous bore with acute Teutonic solemnity, and for the next two and half hours – to my dismay I found that we had taken the stopping train – he drained my vital forces by meandering on about number theory, his prospects of a journalistic career and his considerable ability as a pianist (Transistor later told me that he can just about manage 'Chopsticks'). The other night he was as ponderous as ever, but was dressed for some reason in a nigger-minstrel's outfit and had a crew cut. Transistor's chief virtue as a cook is enthusiasm; she produced a cauliflower-and-nutmeg soup, which could have been used for laying bricks, followed by ratatouille and cake. Unfortunately the language barrier did not prevent her noticing the nudging and eye-catching that accompanied the diners' compliments, and Rackman found her in tears over the cooker. Out of some mixture of malice, altruism and blindness, R had invited Leslie to join us, and I, a weak-minded parrot with a big mouth, heard myself seconding the invitation. Leslie graced the occasion by asking aggressively, 'What, in words of one syllable, is the function of philosophy in society?' – the sort of question that insecure philosophers rehearse answers to in the bath. Having had many such baths over the last twelve years, I was able to make short work of the little chap without answering the question. He abandoned his attack with the orphic utterance, 'The world is about definition.' L is off this week to the Sudan, where, I am encouraged to hear, there is a civil war.

Barbers are usually timid creatures who, if you tell them to cut your hair extremely short, snip off a millimetre and then wait for encouragement, so over the years, in pursuit of a short haircut, I have resorted to increasing hyperbole in my initial instructions. 'Shave it all off!' I shouted gaily to the man in Austin Reed, or words to that effect, and he took me seriously, rushing at the back of my head with a pair of clippers and leaving me looking like an inmate of Treblinka. During the rape of the locks he chatted away, asking me what my job was; I told him I was an antiquarian bookseller, which he took to be someone who sells books about fish. He was obviously delighted with his handiwork: as I gawped in confusion at the diaphanous grey film left on my head, he cried, 'Brilliant! A scholar's haircut!' For the rest of the week I have been the butt of various hurtful comparisons: Old Simpkin told me I looked like a monk, Leslie called me a skinhead (but he is bald and got the obvious rejoinder) and Miss Bochvar said I looked like E.T. The only bonus is that young women, and some young men, keep feeling the nape of my neck, claiming to get a frisson from the bristles.

*

To avoid lining the pockets of Mr Sikorski – whose café serves sandwiches with such fillings as avocado-and-goat-with-truffles or salmon-with-mango-and-bacon – I now make my own sandwiches at Simpkin. Eugenia suggested that I go to Lena's, the *salumeria* in Brewer Street, to try some of their sheep's milk cheese. Lena's is run by fierce Italian men who would put your head on the salami slicer if you insulted their mother, so I looked around for the most inoffensive assistant. He turned out to be deaf. 'What sheep cheese do you have?' I asked. 'Cheap cheese?' he replied suspiciously. 'No, sheep: baaaaaah,' I went, and everyone started sniggering at my imitation. The cheese, which was not cheap, makes good sandwiches but is rather salty.

On Tuesday evening I went to the theatre with Rupert Hoare, his wife and a woman who restores lace. Hoare, who runs Simpkin's history department, is thirty-one but has the manner of Lord Whitelaw. He has a braying voice and bellows down the phone, adjusting the volume between ff and ffff, depending on the distance of his interlocutor; when he rings abroad, his colleagues drop their pens, fall off their seats and knock coffee over their desks. Half his conversation with customers turns on the weather, and the rest consists of clichés like, 'I'll leave the ball firmly in your court.' Whether owing to upbringing, social aspiration or a speech impediment, he lets the sound 'ay' do duty for most vowels, greeting you with a blustering 'Hellay!' in the morning and storming at you – his temper is terrifying – for using his taypwriter within earshot of a customer who has come to bay books.

20 June

The Old Dear having gone away for the weekend to attend Adeline's ninety-third birthday party (she, a spring chicken pushing seventy, was to be one of the youngest guests), I was left cat-sitting. Looking after the two Little Dears in the OD's Fulham flat is an unpleasant business, as one has to change their lavatory – a tray in a specially constructed cage on the balcony which they reach through a saloon-bar-style door. Both LDs produce ammoniac urine that would revive you from a swoon, and Winkle, the larger of the two, periodically expels turds that would do credit to a hippopotamus. He always manages to drop them over the edge of the tray, so that the lavatory attendant has to chase them round the balcony with a trowel.

To avoid this I took them (the cats) and Miss Bochvar to Frogs Cottage, where there is a compost heap to defecate on. To have caught Miss B for myself for a whole weekend was a coup, as she leads a frenzied social life, her conversation sounding like the song 'I Went to a Marvellous Party'. Having her at F.C. is in many ways like being there with my mother: both leave me to get on with my work, both lie in bed reading P.D. James, both sing snatches of popular songs and both watch chat shows on the idiot-box. Miss B sat in my mother's chair watching a particularly obnoxious one late on Saturday night, and, when I censoriously kissed her good night, I momentarily thought I was kissing the Old Dear. The OD once said that as soon as I left home I would find a woman to replace her with; B fits the bill perfectly. We spent some of the weekend talking vaguely about getting married, and agreed on what we desired from married life. Since, however, each of us sees the ideal marriage as barely distinguishable from the lives of two hermits, there does not seem much point in popping the question.

On Saturday morning we went shopping in Knatworth. Knatworth is an overspill town four miles away, which doubles in size once every five years; we shall sell up when its housing estates appear over the hill. Its denizens are uprooted East Enders, the men either unemployed or doing something depressing in light industry, the women pushing what are now, it seems, called 'buggies' containing urchins with overdeveloped larynxes. Young male Knatworthies enjoy themselves by pouring tomato ketchup over old ladies before raping them and stealing their savings; the chief delights of the older folk are looking martyred and standing in queues – pastimes they frequently combine. Miss B and I were twice reprimanded for queue-jumping; once in the bakers, where there were two women behind the counter, one of them serving the members of a long queue in turn, the other standing idle. B and I walked up to the latter and someone in the line barked, 'There's a queue over here, you know.' 'That's why we've come over here,' I wished I had retorted as we drove home. It is best for a product of public school to keep a low profile in Knatworth. Once I accompanied the Old Dear into Boots, where she spent hours dithering over makeup. 'Sacré bleu,' I muttered to myself, and was surprised a few seconds later to hear the same words being uttered in a mock Leo McKern voice, accompanied by gales of derisive laughter, by some bruisers behind the toothpaste shelves.

The other day, I strolled into Simpkin's science department and overheard another conversational gem to treasure along with the discussions about *Auld Lang Syne* and the invention of the pencil-sharpener (v. 11 April). Maurice Montague raised the following question: Can a book of human anatomy contain lifesize illustrations of all the bones in the body, or do we have bones that are longer than a folio volume? I said that to hear a remark like that would dissuade any normal person from a career in bookselling, and was hounded from the room. I must congratulate myself on having performed the feat, hitherto assumed impossible, of making Hank Dreben laugh. Hank, a forty-five-year-old American employee with a dewlap, has the knack of making you feel an idiot, his trick being simply to say nothing. You go up to his desk to ask him a question, and he just stares at you; so you amplify the question or start talking about something else, and end up babbling like a lunatic under his basilisk's gaze. If he does venture a proposition, it will be prefaced by 'Oh, uh'. Eugenia was telling him about a greave, given by an Arabian prince as a present to console a man whose brother he had murdered. I suggested that the present would stop the man from grieving, and Hank made a gurgling noise. Little Moses is becoming increasingly sullen and contumacious in his work, refusing this week to take some books into stock. His head shook with anger as he claimed, falsely, that he had better things to do. The trouble with hiring a friend as an assistant to do jobs that are beneath him is that he soon becomes resentful and uses the fact that he is a chum to try and wriggle out of them. He will have to go.

27 June

It being Book Fair week, the city was alive with visiting firemen, and on Monday evening I took one of them, Justin Myro, out to dinner. He is in his mid-thirties, wears silk harem pants and spectacles with green rims, sports a miniature pigtail and specializes in books on sociology, conducting his business from a villa outside Miami. Myro is a lapsed philosopher and likes to sound off about the iconic value of old books. On his last trip to London he suggested that Maurice and I meet him for breakfast at his hotel. I foolishly left the arrangements to Maurice, who fixed the appointment for 8.00 a.m., unaware, presumably, that if a resident of Catford is to get to Knightsbridge by that hour there is no point in his going to bed the night before. I hired a mini-cab for 7.30 a.m.; the Turk who drove it whizzed expertly through the housing estates of New Cross to avoid the traffic, but had only the vaguest knowledge of central London. 'Knightsbridge?' he said, 'yeah, I've heard of it.' I arrived

47

in time to see the waiter clear away Maurice's kipper bones and a few crispy remains of Myro's fried eggs turned over light, and in the conversation over my smoked haddock it emerged (a) that Maurice thinks that in a few years the Japanese will control the Western World by computer and (b) that all three of us want to be monks.

This time we had dinner at l'Escargot, and I invited Rupert and Laura Hoare for support. RH and I went directly from Simpkin and so arrived an hour early; by the time the other two arrived, we had drunk so many cocktails that we could only talk through clenched teeth and smile idiotically. While we waited, we changed tables three times: first, I objected that our table was too near the piano, so the waiter moved us to a transitional table until another was ready; but the table he prepared for us was over the kitchen's ventilating system, and RH said that the vibration would make him feel sick; so we ended up where we had started and had an earful of tinkling rubbish.

On Tuesday I had lunch with Jonathan Gelberg, who has been a friend since we were thirteen. He is now something important in a merchant bank and, like many successful professionals of his age with interesting, demanding, highly paid jobs and excellent prospects, he whinges about wasting his life. Over lunch he said that he wanted his life to be a 'moral statement' – which I did not understand – and that he yearned to do something useful, but did not explain why he thought being a banker was not useful. Once before, when I asked him what would make him feel useful, he said that he would like to go into politics but that he did not know which party to join. Now, however, he has decided to become a Liberal. I was reminded of the man in Monty Python who says that he always had a burning desire to serve people and that this is why he has become a waiter. Jonathan has always been concerned about the moral and religious dimensions of his life. At school he was in charge of the Jewish Society and would put up notices saying when he rabbi was going to visit; someone would always add a 't' to 'rabbi'. The rabbi was the butt of various practical jokes. Once some anti-semitic lout attached a kipper to the exhaust pipe of the rabbi's car; the thought was that as he drove along, he would start smelling burnt fish and would open the windows to get rid of the smell, thereby causing more of it to waft in.

After school Jonathan went to a yeshiva, where his religious commitment became rabid. During this time he visited me at Oxford and, while we were sitting in my room, he asked me where the East was. When I had worked it out, he produced a bottle of wine, stood up, faced the East and started intoning in Hebrew, occasionally taking swigs from the bottle. When he came up to Oxford a year later, his observance of the law became less strict as I, Abram and others dragged him into a life of dissipation. But he was saved from utter depravity by Rachel, a prim Jewish Mama *in posse* – now his wife and a JM *in esse* – who would complain about his friends using his sitting-room as a brothel/doss-house. Having collapsed on his sofa one night, I awoke the following morning to hear her shriek, 'I'm not going in there till he has his trousers on!' She was also displeased when she walked in to find Abram copulating with someone under the coffee-table. Rachel was then a music student; I first met her in surreal circumstances, when I opened the door of Jonathan's lavatory and found her sitting on the jakes playing the cello. At that stage, for reasons I have never cared to investigate, she thought I was a homosexual rival for J's affections. She none the less agreed to my being best man at their wedding, and I had to hire a morning suit from Moss Bros for the occasion. I did not take any care about choosing the top hat, as no-one ever wears them and I had a velvet cappel to wear in the synagogue; but when I arrived for the ceremony I was told that those, such as the best man, who were to have an active role should wear their top hat rather than a cappel. I just managed to squeeze it on, and while the happy pair were being united I started feeling faint as it dug a trench into my forehead. I became hotter and hotter, warming up the caked sweat deposited in the morning coat's armpits by the previous occupants, and had to spend the rest of the day with my arms pressed to my sides. The service was conducted by a rabbi with a menacing row of teeth and a mellifluous Morningside accent, and was marred only by the incompetence of the organist, who tacked together snatches of tunes, lurching halfway through Mendelssohn's wedding march into the third movement of Beethoven's Fifth. I was dismayed to find that the best man was expected to tip all the synagogue's staff and, being broke at the time, had to appeal to the groom's father to bail me out. We then all drove to the bride's mother's house in Surrey, where we gorged ourselves on a kosher spread provided by one Brett Gubbins. Even the champagne was kosher, i.e. cost twice as much as usual and had been blessed by some rabbi with a sinecure on the Rothschild estate. A marquee had been put up on the lawn and, as the garden had a one-in-five gradient, half the guests periodically fell backwards off their chairs while the other half watched their plates slide away from them across the table. Abram and I plied Rachel with champagne cocktails fortified with sherry, as a result of which – Jonathan reproachfully told us later – she spent the wedding night in a deep sleep.

They have now lived for some years in a detached house in Golders Green and have four young children. Till recently I and a group of fellow-students used to go there fortnightly to discuss philosophy and eat the Gelbergs' biscuits. Rachel, feeling excluded, resented these meetings and used to find ways to interrupt them. Once, after they had been living there for about five years, she came in to ask Jonathan how the record player worked; another time, when we were in the garden, she decided to water the flowers and soaked us all with the hose. Her most devilish act of sabotage – which Jonathan must have connived at – was not to warn us that one of the children had chicken-pox; indeed, I suspect she left a scab on the sofa. Two weeks later I erupted in a rash and still have dents in my neck and forehead. Our meetings were usually in the children's playroom; to strike back, we all smoked heavily – I usually brought a cigar – leaving her and the little ones to choke in a miasma.

We are nevertheless on terms of politeness, and recently she even let Jonathan ask me to Sunday lunch. This was my first encounter with Gelberg family life, as the nippers were always in bed when the *Kreis* arrived. (Jonathan displayed each child for the philosophers' inspection when it was newborn, but then Rachel whisked it out of reach, for fear that we would use it in some experiment.) The two parents practise the 'Nice Man, Nasty Man' technique used by interrogation officers during the war to brainwash their victims: Jonathan is weak and indulgent, letting the little dears do what they like, and then Rachel pounces on them for misbehaviour. After lunch J and I took the children for a walk in Golders Hill Park, J's main purpose being to smoke as many cigarettes as he could while out of Rachel's reach. I was therefore given the pram, and discovered that pram pushing demands considerable skill; the infant inside swayed violently as I negotiated kerb-stones and crazy paving, but was uncomplaining. The ambulatory offspring ran amuck, unrestrained by their father, picking flowers and running on forbidden lawns while passers-by exclaimed 'You are very naughty!' and looked accusingly at me. My experiences that afternoon have made me hesitate to accept Jonathan's invitation at lunch this week to go with them in August to their country seat in Scotland. Another reason for not going is that J's brother may be there with his 'girlfriend', a transsexual J refers to as 'it'.

I am having an affair with an Older Woman, Ellénore, a divorcee of thirty-eight. She has two children, one away at school, the other, call Augustus, a four-year-old with insomnia: he appeared at more than one embarrassing moment in the evening, but seemed uperturbed by what he saw and chattered nonchalantly about the possibility of my staying the night. I had intended to stay after the last train to Catford, but to sleep at my mother's flat in Fulham. However, some spooning in the course of eating a chocolate truffle made a mess of my shirt, so I had to trudge south-eastwards in order to have a clean one in the morning. I should not like Miss Bochvar to know of this liaison, though she gives me so little of her time that it should hardly surprise her.

4 July

Like many elderly ladies, the Old Dear has a strong sentimental interest in cats. I mentioned to her recently that some kittens come and play around Rackman's feet while he digs the garden, and she immediately asserted that they must be rescued, forcing me to give R the phone number of a cat lady who would 'home' them. What they must be rescued *from* is obscure. Fortunately she did not pursue the matter, as she and the cat lady are busy trying to rescue some kittens from the garden of the ground floor flat in the OD's block. She asked the owner of the flat – an uncouth unemployee – whether he would mind their setting a trap, and he grudgingly gave permission. So one evening, when he was off at the pub, the two old souls erected their fiendish device behind the hollyhocks – a cage containing a tempting delicacy and having a portcullis which the intrepid hunters, hiding some yards away in the foliage, could shut behind the unsuspecting feline gourmet by pulling a piece of string. However, before any of the kittens had time to meet with its enforced rescue, the man returned. By his fifth pint he had lost sympathy with the project, and kicked the portcullis down as he went past. The cat lady emerged from the privet, asked him in a quavering voice what he had done that for, and met with some abuse which I will spare the reader. The Old Dear then remonstrated, 'We have to get them in the cage, so we can home them.' 'I'll put you in a bloody cage!' the man warned, and the hunt was abandoned. Since then the OD has been nervous about going past the man's door, in case he carries out his threat.

Last Saturday she had her Level 2 tap dancing exam. She had been nervous about the team display as, in the dress rehearsal, when the rest of the line pranced off to the left, she, gaily waving her bowler hat, went clicking away to the right, ending up some yards from the group. But on the day, in the congenial atmosphere of the Mitcham Adult Education Institute and with the former pianist of the Harry Roy Band as accompanist, her performance was a triumph and she was Highly Commended – though she confided that, when she saw who else was highly commended, she felt like the old codgers who handed in their MBEs when the Beatles were given them.

The tap dancing preventing her from going to the country, I drove up alone on Friday evening. I could have had a pleasant solitary weekend mowing the lawn and reading *Clarissa*, but for some reason invited Abram. A refused to take the Saturday morning bus to Knatworth, forcing me to drive the eighteen miles to Dunham to meet him off the train. His main objection to the bus journey is that it takes three hours while the train usually takes less than two, so I was pleased when he rang to tell me that he would be five and a half hours late as there were engineering works on the line. As it turned out, part of his marathon journey had to be made by a special bus, which he shared with a party of mentally and physically handicapped black people, one of whom collapsed en route. To impress me, Abram brought with him a portable computer, writing on it an article about genetic engineering which he then transmitted down the telephone to *World Affairs Magazine*, doubtless to meet a Sunday mid-afternoon deadline. The cat showed more interest in this gimmick than I did and walked over the keyboard as the message was going down the line, so readers of *World Affairs Magazine* should expect some aleatory interpolations on next week's science page.

On Monday the strain of keeping the secret that I am leaving Simpkin finally proved too much, and I divulged it to Old Simpkin. By the time it had spread through the shop, each of my colleagues had come up to tell me what a good idea it was to leave the world of old books. Stitt, the last obstacle removed from his road to empire, showed laudable self-control, managing not to dance a hornpipe – at least not in front of me. Although, by a reflex of self-deprecation, I have always denied that I am any good at bookselling, I shall in fact be a loss to the philosophy department, as my literacy, erudition and intellectual power are a complement to Stitt's hustling skills. Old Simpkin was right, when I broke the news, to express fear for the standard of cataloguing, as Stitt, though a former student of modern languages, has only the faintest grasp of syntax, or for that matter semantics and pragmatics, and his descriptions of books often lapse into gibberish.

That evening I went with a party to a concert of twentieth century songs, part of the Almeida Festival. The Almeida Theatre is alleged to have the highest proportion of Ph.D.s among its audiences; I used to go from wishful thinking, and now go to keep up the statistics. The party comprised little Moses, Judy, Louise and Fleur Duprat – Simpkin's recent French acquisition, an archetypal Parisienne of thirty-five with a pointed face, billows of scent and an infinite wardrobe. Though she has now been working in the shop some months, she has appeared in a new outfit every day; Eugenia's theory is that she lives near an Oxfam shop and keeps swapping her clothes there. She has now taken charge of the art department and bustles about like Mrs Thatcher, venomously spitting 'Merci infiniment!' down the phone and speaking English with an alarming French/American accent ('Sotheby's' becomes 'Sozzebee', and 'huge' becomes 'yoosh'). In another month or so she will be a battleaxe. Further to the list of Simpkin anecdotes: Moses proposed, for a reason that escapes me, that our books should carry a 'sell by' label.

19 July

Surprise parties are a bad idea, because the best bit of a party is the period of anticipation. They also cause trouble to those who have to keep the secret from the victim; I once spent a morning in Oxford presenting Abram with increasingly flimsy reasons for going for walks, to prevent him from discovering some nascent festivities in his room. A fortnight ago Rachel arranged for sixteen people to surprise Jonathan on his thirtieth birthday. We were told to meet at Rothschild's, a kosher Chinese restaurant in Blandford Street (there is another branch, probably more popular, in Hendon). The waiters didn't look Jewish, and in fact the restaurant was much like any other Chinese, except that the food was half as good and twice as expensive and most of the male diners wore hats. Jonathan's face fell when he was greeted by a self-conscious chorus of 'Happy Birthday To You', and he spent much of the meal in bemused silence as the guests – mainly Rachel's girlfriends and their husbands – prattled about babies, cars and household appliances. At one point he started a discussion with me about the nature of rationality, but Rachel would have none of it and, in the course of trying to kick him under the table, bruised the shins of four other members of the party. After the second course J and I were separated, as everyone was made to move two places to the left. 'Boy, have you picked the short straw!' said the man who ended up opposite me. He was right.

Rebecca came to Frogs Cottage for the weekend. There is only one walk there, so we went on it twice. The first time we stopped to lie in the grass, where we indulged in some pleasing mutual exploration till interrupted by a dog. 'He's too affectionate,' the owner said; it was unclear whom he was referring to. The second time R was peevish and said that all public-school boys are emotional cripples. I replied that it depends on your criterion of emotional health, and pointed to a couple of geese we were passing as the sort of paradigm she might have in mind. This resulted in a tight-lipped silence. R seems tired of me and made various remarks implying that she wants our affair to end. 'I think I'll marry a foundling,' she said apropos some supposed manifestation of an Oedipus complex by me, and 'I did enjoy our holiday in Greece,' in a manner suggesting that it was an event in the distant past. Edie will be sad: 'I like your girlfriend; do you?' she said after coming for a drink. On the Saturday evening R and I went to a party given by a friend of hers in Cambridge. The friend's mother, a woman of sixty-five, had just remarried. 'Have you seen my new little husband?' she asked, as if referring to a Jack Russell or a kitchen gadget. 'Here he is; isn't he sweet?' And the little chap smiled and nodded and went off to find drinks. I was disheartened to discover that he is a solicitor.

Returning morosely to the Empire Road Monastery on Sunday evening, I was cheered by a call from Ellénore proposing that I stay the night with her after the opera the following day. E's story is a sad one – her husband, a mentally unstable stockbroker, walked out just after the birth of their second son and refused to give her any money – but she has the warmth of a blast furnace. It is hard to know why she puts up with someone like me, who looks at life through the wrong end of a telescope. Our first night together was an emotional laxative, and I also received some anatomical lessons about fifteen years overdue. Her mother lives next door to Dr Daniel Hopkin, who, in our affluent days, was our GP. I remember Hopkin as a gentle, soft-spoken man with a twenty-four-hour five o'clock shadow (my father, also hispid, once recommended him a special razor with two blades). Evidently he was a fiend in disguise, for E's ma has repeatedly heard women's screams from her neighbour's house, once catching the words, 'Don't touch me! If you come nearer, I'll kill you!'

Following the atmosphere of finality that Rebecca had cast over the weekend, I was surprised to be invited by her to dinner on Friday. A flagging Don Giovanni, I dragged myself on to the East London line (part of the tube being flooded) and reached her flat in Islington in about the time it would have taken to get to Samarkand. During a stilted conversation, I was stung on the hand by a wasp which, after I had trodden on it and torn it wing from wing, I thought no more about until I started itching all over. Coming over queer, I went off to be sick, caught a glimpse of my face, puffy and contorted, in the bathroom mirror, and then passed out on the stairs. In a brief moment of lucidity, I reminded R that Max Stirner, champion of the sovereign ego, had died from a gnat bite, and she dialled 999. The pair of us were whisked in an ambulance to a seedy casualty unit somewhere near Archway, the ambulanceman remarking on the way, 'It's carnage in there tonight.' R was directed to a waiting-room where a drunk woman smelling of pee, with a bleeding gash across her skull, asked her for some money for a bag of chips. I meanwhile was laid on a couch behind a curtain, and a student nurse felt my

57

pulse. She told me she could not detect any heartbeat, which alarmed me; but, deciding presumably that this reflected more on her competence than on my health, she strolled off without ringing any alarms. I lay there for half an hour, listening to the duty doctor dealing with the case the other side of the curtain, a man who had attempted suicide. The doctor told him perfunctorily not to do it again, and then went off to fetch a stomach pump, saying jokingly to a nurse, 'I started off with a caring attitude, but I grew out of it in a week.' The doctor who finally saw me was a Dutch woman with little grasp of English. She gave me a bottle with four antihistamine pills in it and a label saying, 'Take two pills a day for three days.' I was then discharged, and Rebecca, clearly inferring to hypochondria from the fact that I was now able to stand, took me back to her flat, putting me in her absent flatmate's bed, with a bucket within mouth's reach. My hand and – for some reason – my knob are still puffy and I have been feeling delicate. So delicate, in fact, that all I can remember of my reunion last night with my Scottish friend Hamish, who is on a brief visit from Hamburg, where he now lives, is that he has started saying 'Ach' instead of 'Och'.

25 July

On Wednesday, having told Rackman to be on his best behaviour, I gave a dinner party for grown-ups at Empire Road. The Old Dear had dictated a Jocelyn Dimbleby recipe down the phone; as she read out the instructions she kept adding scholia like 'But of course I wouldn't do that,' or 'You could use salt instead,' so that in the end I was floundering and barked that I refused to accept contradictory orders. I took the afternoon off to buy and cook, but in fact spent most of it asleep, and so was in a state of frenzy when Anthony Monaghan arrived one and a half hours early. He is an old friend of

Derek Badham's father, and Derek recently gave him a rather menial job. A distinguished-looking man in his sixties, the grandeur of his manner is grossly disproportionate to the lowliness of his responsibilities, the explanation being alcoholism, which has prevented him from ever holding down a job for longer than the space between bouts. Recently he went to stay with Derek and, after an evening's boozing, staggered off to bed. Derek also turned in, but was awakened by the phone three hours later; it was the police, saying that they had just found a car, containing a drunken Mr Monaghan, in a ditch, and would Mr Badham please come and take Mr Monaghan home. The car was Derek's; Anthony, in a reverie in bed, had decided that it would be pleasant to get up and take it for a night-time spin. He was contrite but Derek shouted for a week about the expense of spirit in a waste of shame. As Anthony walked up Empire Road eating some peanuts, a couple of youths shouted 'Monkey' at him. 'Piss off,' he replied drily, but let them have the last word, viz 'Bald wanker.' Since Anthony has a full head of hair, this was a puzzling insult, but apparently they had been on the lighter fuel. Next to arrive, as I continued trying to disentangle the recipe, was Ellénore, who brought a zabaglione but did not bring Eugenia and Alec ffiske, whom she was supposed to collect. After an acrimonious phone conversation, they set off in a mini-cab, arriving shortly before ten o'clock. Poor Leslie, whom I had banished from the kitchen till I had served, was wilting with inanition by the time he had leave to open his tin of sardines. Some of my guests thought it was sad that he should be eating convenience food alone in the room next door, so I had to deliver a speech about sentimentality. The party was agreeable, though there was a distressing round of anecdotes about being sick and Eugenia told a story of a man whose feet started bleeding at a dinner. (Rackman muttered 'Pus in boots'.)

*

On arrival at Goose End last night, I was given the latest news about Edie. The Old Dear had gone round to see her in the afternoon and found her lying on her back on the floor without trousers or skirt. A doctor was sent for who turned out to be an expert in crumblies, and as he examined Edie he asked her various leading questions to test her memory. He soon discovered that she had enough aluminium deposit in her brain to make a set of saucepans. 'There's nothing wrong with my memory,' bleated Edie. 'Why have you asked me my name five times, then?' he retorted unkindly. He then asked her who her neighbours were. 'Well, there's Lady North,' she began. The doc didn't believe a word of this. 'Lady North! Who's Lady North?' 'I am,' snapped the Old Dear, who had been listening behind the door with Mr Bird. The doctor still looked unconvinced, the OD wearing unladylike gardening clothes. While the examination was in progress, the OD and Bird discovered five tumblers smelling of sherry on Edie's sitting-room table. These, combined with the fact that the poor old thing eats nothing, presumably explained her supine state. As the OD and I sat down to dinner at 9.00 p.m., Bird banged on the back door. 'She's gone!' he cried, having just seen Edie's Mini disappear into the dusk. When E returned about an hour later, she was trembly and the OD had to put her to bed. 'I've done such a silly thing,' E said, as the OD, trying to avert her gaze, was helping her off with her clothes. 'I've just been to the shops, but they were all shut.' The OD was about to reply, 'Of course they were shut, you old idiot, it's ten o'clock on a Friday evening!' but Edie continued, 'You see, it's Wednesday afternoon – early closing.'

1 August

This week Len Breens, the packer at Simpkin, returned to work, having been run over some months ago. Sixty years old, five foot two inches high, with a bald head, twinkling eyes and stubbly face, he looks like a character from *Endgame*, appearing on Monday in a soiled raincoat that reached down to his bare calves (he was wearing shorts). His clothes are always eccentric and, because he rides a bicycle, he changes them frequently – though not, it seems, for reasons of hygiene, as he gives off a strong smell. (He has a bath once a week, on Friday nights.) The changes are leisurely affairs, and he strolls round the packing-room trouserless and pantsless, his Johnson swinging like a farm animal's, frightening the female employees. Len's work is accompanied by a warbling whistle and belches from the pit of the stomach; Geoffrey Denley told him off for breaking wind in the sales area, so he now tries to restrict it to the basement. This however is a small concession, for the noises he makes are so loud that they can still be heard upstairs by the customers. In any case he frequently forgets himself. 'Arlp,' he went recently in front of an elderly academic, followed by, 'Oops, sorry, guvnor.' His accent is one of the last examples of perfect cockney and should be recorded – with belches too – for the BBC sound archives. Len also likes to spit, and the wall around his work table is encrusted with gobbets which give off a stench in the summer. There is dried spittle too on the receiver of the packing-room's telephone; seasoned employees refuse to take calls there. His behaviour in the lavatory is noteworthy. Above the shop's urinal, at a height of about five feet, there is a small metal box with a grille – some kind of disinfecting mechanism. Len, if he has an audience, will pretend that the box is a microphone and croon 'Why, why, why, Delilah' down it while peeing. And, when he is at stool, he sits on the jakes back to front; I know this because the partition dividing the WC from the rest of the washroom only comes to within nine inches of the floor, and I have seen Len's feet facing the wrong way. Not surprisingly he is kept as far away from customers as possible, though sometimes acciden-tal meetings take place. Professor Kenji Nakayama,

Distinguished Professor of European History at Heikko University, arrived by mistake at the trade entrance and was let in by Len: 'It's mister Nackywatsit!' Len shouted as the professor grinned and bowed at him.

Len is assisted by Jesus, a Spaniard with a foot each side of the sanity line, who tries to conceal a murderous temper under jittery, hand-wringing obsequiousness. If you pass him in the corridor or walk over the floor he is washing, he will press himself to the wall in the attitude of his namesake on the cross and babble, 'Thank you, thank you'; if you ask him to empty a wastepaper basket, he will pounce on it while murmuring, his voice quavering with reverence, 'I do it, I do it, now, now, now.' Jesus can't bear anyone to be standing at the urinal while he is cleaning the men's lavatory, and rushes out as soon as anyone walks in. In consequence all the men in Simpkin are disposed to Jesus-like behaviour: if, as they are walking into the gents, they see him in there with a mop, they rush out again to prevent him from doing so. It is not hard to conjure the demon from inside the rabbit: someone misguidedly complained about the state of the ladies' lavatory, and Jesus tore in, grinding his teeth and growling, 'I clean, I clean.' When he had finished, he put a large sign on the door of the ladies', saying NOW IS CLEAN, and went home in a rage to Uxbridge, where he lives with his eight sisters. He derives consolation from animals. The old easy-chair which he sits in during his breaks is infested with mice, and as he drinks his coffee he reaches under the cushion, pulling out a mouse and letting it run over his legs. He found a rat in the gents and told Maurice how sweet it was. When Maurice sent for the rat man (actually a rat lady, six foot high and wearing a helmet), Jesus called M a silly cow and never forgave him.

While Len was away, Jesus became sentimental about him, promising 'I look after my fren Len', and on Len's return he called him to his face 'poor little man'. But it will not be long before Len is driving him to distraction, particularly as it is now August and the wall is warming up. Shortly before Len's accident I was in the packing-room behind some shelves. In the manner of a problem in decision theory, I knew that both Len and Jesus were there; Jesus (who was just the other side of the shelves, making tea) could not see me, but knew that Len was there; and Len thought he was by himself. Len was at his most extreme, whistling 'White Christmas' with a tremolo worthy of Gwynneth Jones and punctuating the verses with gastric noises, while Jesus writhed with fury over the kettle, emitting a long 'No-o-o-o-o' from the throat. One day the tension became too much and Jesus collapsed, complaining of numbness in the right arm. It was feared that he had had a stroke, so Louise, a falter-ing hispanophone, was detailed to take him to the hospi-tal. 'Tell me is no strike, Louise, tell me is no strike!' he pleaded on the way, so she obliged. When they arrived, they were kept waiting for two hours until a sister came and asked Jesus, 'Have you been weighed?' 'I been weighed two hours!' he shouted.

There have been other packers at Simpkin. One, with the innocent name Timmy, was locked up for GBH; he was another of Geoffrey's rough traders. Then there was a huge black man called Albert, also known for his violent temper. My colleague Max Wood decided to use Albert in a practical joke. He rang down to the packing-room and told Albert that Old Simpkin wanted to borrow an axe and would Albert please take one to his office. Then he phoned Old S and told him that Albert had gone berserk with an axe.

8 August

The other day Louise asked me to go with her to a prom concert. We decided to eat first at the Daquise, a café of long standing in which the South Kensington Polish community sit about over glasses of tea or Bison vodka. You always see the same people there: the gaggle of old Polish princesses who have fallen on hard times and sit round the cash register in their diamonds; the Doppelgänger of Janáček; the young man who has read too much Dostoevsky and sits in his knee-length boots, dark glasses and peaked cap, smoking a cigarette and wondering whether to plant an axe in his concierge's head. The Poles like to form clusters; there is alleged to be another group in Ealing. These locations are puzzling, for immigrants are supposed to settle near their port of entry. Perhaps some Polish parachutists landed in South Kensington and Ealing during the war. Louise and I ordered respectively a Polish black pudding and a 'continental sausage', each having a half of each. The reason for our choice was that the dishes are easy to pronounce and the Daquise waitresses are sticklers for pronunciation. I once innocently ordered a Bortsch and was met with a withering stare of feigned incomprehension. After several seconds the waitress smiled pityingly and said, 'Ah, you mean Baartzscjcz!' At prom concerts we are too grand to stand in the arena and too poor not to. So we did, hoping not to be seen by anyone we knew. I was immediately spotted by a man I had recently sat next to at a dinner, but at least he was promenading as well. Louise's *raison d'assister* was to hear the performance of a piece by a schoolfriend, one of the walls-of-sound brigade. It was clear from the piece that he is an undistinguished composer and clear from his appearance, to take a bow, that he is a poofter, which saddened L, who said she had a soft spot for composers.

Last weekend my mother's friend Audrey Flews came to Frogs Cottage. She is seventy-ish, bluff, strikingly ugly and drawls in a loud voice about her family and other tedious topics. I accompanied her from London on Friday evening, and in the rush hour tube she brayed that she couldn't understand why anyone worked in London. 'They have to eat,' I mumbled, hoping to deflect the glares of commuters from over their *Standards*. 'I'd rather stay in the country and eat grass,' she yelled. It is depressing how little correlation there is between the degree of conviction with which someone holds a belief and the degree of precision that the belief's content has. Audrey has a wide range of vague and reactionary views which are so entrenched that she takes them for matters of uncontroversial fact. Over dinner on Saturday she and the Old Dear indulged in a tiresome jeremiad, allegedly on aesthetic grounds, against 'declining' standards of English pronunciation. I tried to put a stop to it by accusing them of rationalizing their insecurity about their social position. 'Rot!' Audrey barked.

Addendum for readers following the decline of Edie Fawcett: while I was mowing the lawn, she came up and said, 'I don't know what to do, there's a little grey cat asleep in my house. It isn't mine, and I don't know how it got there. Do come and look.' It was of course Lupin, the cat she has lived with for the past thirteen years – her only friend. I gave him a positive identification, but Edie seemed unconvinced. This week she was certified by a specialist to be (as we doctors say) off her trolley.

15 August

Our family Christmases have become increasingly dreary over the years, the personnel for the dinner now usually consisting solely of me, the Old Dear and Edie, who in her senility has almost stopped bringing presents. One year she produced a bottle of Liebfraumilch (with the £1.85 label still on it) in return for the gifts we showered upon her. Whether it is worth showering gifts on her is doubtful, for she immediately forgets she has received them. One of my presents to her was a bottle of Madeira. On Boxing Day we went to her house for a drink, and she produced this bottle, saying with distaste, 'I don't know if this is drinkable; I bought it in Knatworth.' The bottle carried a large Fortnum and Mason label. Last year but one, my mother decided that the rot had gone far enough, so to enliven the proceedings she invited a man with terminal cancer and his wife and daughter. The man, Reginald Holmes, was implausibly merry, cracking quips beginning 'When I've copped it', while his wife and daughter looked tearful, the OD and I looked round the room in embarrassment and Edie gobbled away oblivious. Reginald has now copped it, and was cremated at Putney Vale East Chapel. His ashes were to be transported to Wiltshire to take part in a memorial service near the Holmes's country house, so Julia, Holmes *fille*, went round to the undertakers to choose an urn. She found those on offer repulsive, and so set off to Liberty's to find a more appealing one. Unfortunately the elegant vessel she chose did not have a screw top, so she and her mother were worried that Reginald would blow away as they drove down the M3. At least he fitted into a small space, the Putney Vale incinerator having a high temperature. Rebecca, when she was in India, met a couple of old English ladies who were on holiday. One of them died in Bombay and was cremated there, and her relations asked for her ashes to be flown home to England. The Bombay oven was more suitable for meringues than for corpses, and the deceased's ashes – and presumably pieces of charred bone and shrivelled flesh – filled several sacks. Her companion was charged for excess baggage on the return flight. Care must be taken when scattering ashes. The mother of Moll McPhail, a schoolfriend, left instructions in her will that her ashes be scattered in the sea off Bournemouth. Moll's father hired a boat and drank several whiskies to steady his nerves on the painful occasion. The whiskies unsteadied his balance, however, and as he was scattering his wife's ashes he slipped on the deck and broke his back. Dr McPhail is accident prone. Convalescing after months in plaster, he went for a walk and, as he was crossing the road between two parked cars, one of them sprang into reverse, breaking the doctor's legs between the bumpers. He is now mentally broken as well. A while ago, trying to get in touch with Moll, I rang him up, and he maundered tearfully and drunkenly down the phone till I was forced to hang up, pretending that we had been cut off. He used to have a practice in Harley Street and dealt mainly with Arabs. What his speciality was, I did not like to enquire; once he answered the front door with his arms up to the elbows in blood. 'Go on through,' he cried breezily, 'I'll join you in a minute.' As well as Moll, he had two daughters called Poll and Doll. I don't know what became of any of them, though I heard that Moll had become a cab driver in New York.

I was in America myself this week on an executive trip. A prof in the philosophy department at the University of Baltimore was retiring and wanted to flog his extensive library. Being no longer young, I decided to go Club Class. Unfortunately Stitt, who opens everyone's mail at Simpkin, opened the envelope containing my tickets while I was away on holiday. 'I see you've decided to go out in style,' he said down the phone. 'How do you mean?' I replied, knowing very well. 'One Super Club return ticket to Washington for Dr J. North, £1,067.' At this point I should have told Stitt, my junior, to boil his head, but I knew that our otherwise generous boss hates extravagance in tickets and that S would let him know of my modest precaution against extreme discomfort. 'Outrageous!' I cried. 'I wouldn't have ordered a Club ticket if I'd known it would be that much more.' 'Shall I change it to an Economy fare?' Stitt offered helpfully. As a result I had fifteen hours in a Pan Am Sardine Class seat to ponder how to ruin Stitt's career in the two weeks before I leave Simpkin. The plane was packed with holiday-making families. I caught the fancy of an infant in front, who first tried to remove my glasses by reaching his hand between the seats and then gave me a fright by crawling round and pulling my trouser leg. The child's parents were unconcerned, and my glares were otiose. At first I thought I was lucky to have a free place next to me, but, as it was the smoking compartment, people from non-smoking kept asking to sit in it while they had a fag, and I was continually moving books, papers and clothes on to the floor to make room for them. Having churlishly admitted an elderly man with a kindly face, I buried myself fiercely in *An Introduction to English Legal History*. 'Boy, have you got trouble!' he said merrily, catching sight of the title, and babbled about how much easier it was to learn the law by reading thrillers. He may have been right. This is the most boring book but one that I have read; the most boring of all was *The English Legal System*, which should have been sold with free matchsticks for propping open the eyelids. I seem to have made a terrible mistake in choosing a legal career, and ought to know by now not to take turgid books on long flights. After an hour my eyes had drifted to the movie, which I followed with difficulty, having waved away a headset.

In Washington I had dinner twice with my dear friend Julius Bromwell, of whom Abram once said, apparently truly, that he is a man with no faults. He is also huge; Hamish was sitting with Julius in the back of a car, and when the latter breathed in deeply the former thought he was going to be crushed to death. We all know Julius because he was a graduate student of philosophy with us at the University of London. He then went on to Yale law school and is now 'clerking' – or, as he says, 'clurking' – for a judge before moving to a firm where his job will be to defend crooked arms manufacturers against suits brought by the American government. For this he will earn an immense salary, and he already has the sports car to match – a red thing which you have to lie down in. I was embarrassed to get into it when he picked me up at the hotel. We went at his suggestion to a restaurant called Chez Bettine, where the waiter squatted between us and said, 'Hi, I'm Bruce, I'll be servin' you this evening, how ya doin'?' 'Fine,' I answered nervously, trying to avoid his eye (eighteen inches away from my own) and wondering whether etiquette required me to ask him how *he* was doin'. Neither Julius nor I could remember what carpaccio was, so Julius recklessly asked Bruce. Instead of simply telling us that it is thinly sliced smoked beef, B enthusiastically recited a long and word perfect panegyric in which every clause had the intonation of a question: 'Carpaccio is wafer-thin slices of the finest tenderloin beef from the Iowa prairies? slowly and delicately smoked over exquisitely aromatic hickory wood? and served with a complementary garnishing of crisp fresh lettuce? and . . .' After thirty seconds of this, we decided to have the goat's cheese with peppers, but Bruce was not discomfited. 'Sure!' he shrieked with a fanatical beam, 'it's delicious!' The food was good, but Bettine was of the deplorable New Kitchen school, serving main courses the size of an aperitif snack. Returning to my hotel room, I raided the mini-bar for pretzels and plunged on the chocolate mint which the management kindly lay on your pillow with a card saying, 'So glad you're here.' The night before, I had failed to notice the mint and had an earful of soft chocolate in the morning.

To return to Miss Fawcett. My mother now goes round regularly in the morning to get Edie up and give her some breakfast. Last weekend she found E shut in her bedroom – curtains tightly drawn and double-glazed windows locked – with Lupin and Lupin's food bowls and litter tray. E does not care to go to the bathroom at night and does not have a chamberpot, so she pees in a large glass cooking bowl. This was in the room as well, and contained a sample. Nature had obviously called twice during the night, for she had also peed into Lupin's bowl of water. His other bowl contained baked beans and pieces of cheese, for E now finds it hard to distinguish human from feline fare; she was recently found nibbling Go Cat Pilchard Crunchies with her sherry. This reflects a confusion between cats and people. On one occasion Edie's clock broke down and there was some discussion as to who could mend it. 'Is this the man who's come to mend the clock?' she asked, pointing at Lupin. L's litter tray usually lives in E's guest-room but, having brought it into her own room, she had left in the guest-room an empty cardboard box on a piece of newspaper. Before the cat had been locked in with his crazed mistress for the night, he had gone into the guest-room for a pee and, failing to find his usual convenience, emptied his bladder, reasonably enough, into the box. The pee sank through the cardboard and newspaper and impregnated the carpet. Fortunately Miss Fawcett no longer entertains. Most cats in the country have an outdoor lavatory, but Edie, terrified that her companion might be run over, has not let him out of the house for over a year. When reprobated for cruelty, she whimpers, 'I love him very much,' but this is clearly a love that seeketh only self to please. The other day she was discovered pressing the poor beast into a clothes drawer. A notable feature of Edie's senility is a preoccupation with arranging things in patterns: she had arranged her Pilchard Crunchies in arabesques, and my mother and Mr Bird found some rotten fruit placed in a circle on E's dining-table. Bird, a connoisseur in the history of art, remarked, 'Very Piccassio.'

Relief for sufferers from warts: Old Simpkin has for some years had an increasingly large wart in his navel, and was worried that, as in a Kafka story, the wart might eventually swallow him up. He went to a doctor who prescribed a sophisticated ointment which had no effect. Old S remonstrated, and the doctor then suggested that he apply black banana skin to the affected part. He stuck a small piece of skin into his navel, and the wart has indeed started shrinking. The trouble is that, despite his navel's being enveloped by rolls of fat, the banana skin keeps falling out; he complained that his bed is full of small bits of black banana, and warned us yesterday that there is a piece somewhere on the shop floor. He was just off to Boots to find some tape to stick over his navel. I pointed out – as little Moses, who was listening, became increasingly pale – that if his stomach were hairy it would be painful removing the tape to put in a new bit of banana, and Old S mused that he might hire someone to shave it. There were no volunteers.

22 August

An American woman I do not know, called Mary Lou something-or-other, rang up to invite herself to dinner on the inadequate grounds (a) that we both know Julius, (b) that I live in London and (c) that she is in London on holiday. She was clearly aware of the pretext's flimsiness, for her voice trembled as she gave the invitation. She is not, however, naturally diffident, and in Manzi's she drawled deafeningly about venture capital, whatever that is, causing people at other tables to turn round and embarrassing her host. We shared a salmon trout, preceded in my case by an uncuttable piece of smoked eel which showed signs, as I vainly tried to penetrate it, of being about to fly across the table and land in the venture capitalist's lap. Bourbon and Macon played havoc with my syntax, but Mary Lou seemed to find me entertaining, occasionally saying 'That's funny, Joseph' in a deadpan voice. If I had stuck a fish knife in her, she would have said 'That's painful, Joseph' in the same monotone.

On returning to Empire Road, I caught the end of a dinner party given by Rackman, a candidate for the title Dreariest Event in World History. A flabby barrister-turned-solicitor fixed me with his eye, like the Ancient Mariner, and delivered a monologue on a legal point connected with company cars, while his wife smiled in a sickly manner at the floor. In the corner an accountant, as shrivelled as Stephen Hawking, sat in silence, his lips pursed sourly, and – to crown the occasion – there was Leslie, beaming at me across the room. Leslie will be leaving the Hermitage soon, and I shall look back on his discreet little ways with nostalgia, for he is likely to be replaced by a vegetarian female pianist from Australia, accompanied by piano. Pianists are notoriously unstable mentally, and I, who plan to study at home from next month, am hysterically sensitive to noise. Rackman, who, to circumvent my supposed power of veto, managed to interview the woman when I was out, said only that she *may* bring a piano; but this modal operator is clearly the symptom of a weak-minded and devious intent to placate me.

Mary, a former lodger of R's, plays the violin but never practises. She is at present touring Canada with the orchestra, who are trying to keep solvent by playing 'Dig Those Classics' – a medley of familiar tunes from the classical and romantic repertoire accompanied by a disco beat (M wore earplugs while digging, until she was told they could be seen by the audience). She has sent Rackman and me a postcard showing a Mountie shaking hands with a Red Indian, and R, before passing it to me, underlined his name on the address in red to draw atten-tion to the fact that it was written above mine. The ques-tion of priority has caused many jealous scenes, and Mary used to resort to ever more ingenious arrange-ments of our names on her postcards in the hope of maintaining equality. Granted that on posters advertis-ing films the lefthand side is conventionally more honorific than the right, and the top than the bottom, she finally decided to put one of our names halfway down the left side of the card's address section and the other name slightly higher on the right; but this still caused quibbles, so she now writes the names in any old order. To avenge myself on Rackman for the invidious post-card, I have disregarded the written instruction left by Transistor with a melon she delivered to Simpkin when I wasn't there, that I should give half to him; I took the whole thing to the Old Dear's for dinner, but it was not ripe enough to eat. Rackman in any case should stop hankering after Transistor; 'He's so soft!' she confided to me, possibly referring to his spare tyres.

On Friday evening, Old Simpkin being away, those employees who were not on holiday sat around chatting idly, and little Moses and I fell to comparing anecdotes about unusual deaths. The attentive reader of these pages will know already that Max Stirner died of a gnat bite, but does he also know that Scriabin – who was so convinced that he was Jesus Christ that he invited a party of friends to watch him walk on water – died from a mosquito bite on the lip? Another composer who met a bizarre end was Félix Alkan: he was climbing a ladder to reach a Talmud from the top of his bookcase when the shelves came away from the wall, pushed the ladder backwards and crushed him. I suggested to the little chap that we publish an anthology of deaths, if it has not been done already; there is already one of last words. I hope this will not encourage Moses to add Louise and me to the list; we are going to his flat for dinner next Tues-day, and he has been experimenting with recipes. Already we have had one lucky escape: he tried making a cabbage-and-egg pie, but fortunately was dissatisfied with it.

The latest news of Edie is also culinary. My mother looked into Edie's fridge and found a small bathroom sponge, buttered and sitting on a plate. She intends to refuse any invitation from Edie to tea. E is certainly not one of those old people who do not receive a regular visitor. Another neighbour, Brenda Runeckles (a widow in her fifties, with whom Bird is besotted), had grandchildren staying with her and looked in on Edie twice, first with her youngest grandchild, a babe in arms, and the following day with a slightly older one, a toddler. 'Goodness, how quickly he's grown!' exclaimed Edie on the second visit. Brenda lives in a bungalow down the road, whose name, engraved on a varnished cross-section of a tree hanging from a wrought-iron frame, is 'Bonker's'. It was given this name by its previous occupants, who had decided they were bonkers to live there. Brenda and her husband bought it as a retirement home, but he dropped dead on the day of the move, which caused the Old Dear to make some tasteless speculations about the corpse's being transported in the removal van. The sudden death did not surprise Abram, who remarked that moving house is widely recognized to be one of the most stress-creating events in people's lives. But he is ill qualified to pronounce on this, having lived in a state of ataraxia in the same house since he was born.

31 August

Following the failure of the experimental cabbage-and-egg pie, Moses decided to serve spinach soup, stuffed marrow, salad, torta di dolcelatte and chocolate digestive biscuits. He had taken trouble, and it was all good except the marrow, whose stuffing tasted of dry rot. Louise, Judy, Moses and I sat at the little fellow's desk, dragged from under his home computer and placed in the sitting-room. To eat from a regular table is a rare honour at 35 Aneurin Bevan House. Once when I dined there we huddled round on old treadle table for a sewing machine; whenever we moved our feet, a large cast-iron wheel started spinning at the side. The last time, when M and I were eating alone, he merely drew two easy chairs up to the gas fire and we balanced our bowls of soup on the arms; this might have been *gemütlich* enough, except that I was in the lefthand chair and M insisted on placing his soup on the right-hand arm of his chair, so that he was facing away from me throughout the meal. The chocolate biscuits would have been followed by melon, but by this time we were bloated; Louise and I had eaten so much that we had to lie down on a mattress conveniently placed by the table. I wish I had not recommended *Auto da Fé* to Moses, as it has given him even more bad ideas. When we had digested enough to be able to speak again, he quoted, with merriment and apparent approval, the remark made by the loutish concierge Pfaff, 'All women should be beaten to death.' Judy, who believes everything the little chap says, smiled in apparent agreement.

I was late for dinner, because, just as I was leaving Simpkin, the Old Dear rang up in a state, begging me to go to Fulham on the way, to feed her cats. She had gone to Goose End for the day to see Edie's niece and sister-in-law – who, not having been near Edie for years, were visiting her to assess the degree of her decline – and was trapped there by floods. 'The little dears haven't had anything to eat since breakfast,' the OD whined tearfully, as I remained sullen and monosyllabic, 'they'll be desperate!' The little dears are spherical and could only benefit from missing a meal. When I had got the porter to let me into the flat, I found them drowsy and serene, and lectured them about sentimentality and anthropomorphism.

On Friday evening I visited Eugenia ffiske. She lives in Phillimore Gardens with her husband Alec, and their son Cecil stays there intermittently. Alec is an art dealer with a dry sense of humour; at a *vernissage* where a gaggle of aesthetes were effusing over a still life with potatoes, he remarked, 'Yes, the eyes follow you round the room.' Eugenia dotes on Cecil, a gangling creature of twenty-six who looks like a stork. After he left Eton he formed a rock band called Killer Hertz and was then given a clerical job at Simpkin. While he was there he made a lot of noise but never uttered a sentence – just the occasional monosyllable and a lot of cheerful phonemes: 'Ay, eh, right, oy!' When once I bumped into him in the Dainty Café, I thought I would be bound to hear him say something meaningful as he ordered his sandwiches, but he just went, 'Ah, ee, ay, yeah!' and the lady behind the counter replied, 'Your usual, Cecil,' in an understanding voice. The Dainty smells over-poweringly of vinegar and fat, and every sandwich contains a hair. The fillings are put into the sandwiches with a small number of spoons, so you often find a bit of liver sausage in with your prawn and cream cheese. It is run, of course, by an Italian family – an unshaven man with a match between his teeth, and his two barely distinguishable sisters who call you 'Boss' and 'Darling', often in the same sentence. The café's trade has dwindled with the rise of the beluga-and-kiwifruit school of sandwich bar, and one by one its Simpkin regulars have deserted it for Sikorski's. One day when, deterred by the Sikorski queue, I returned to the Dainty, I was greeted with a stony glare and served without a single 'Boss' or 'Darling'.

A couple of years ago Cecil had tonsilitis and went to the doctor. Looking down his throat, the doctor reeled back at the size of his larynx and advised him to take up an operatic career. Since then he has been training in Rome with a famous baritone, who I think he said was called Salieri. When Cecil looked into Simpkin recently, I asked him to give us a blast, but then changed my mind, fearing he might frighten the older customers. Unabashed, he went into the street and bellowed 'Se vuol ballare' through the window. It sounded operatic enough over the traffic. He has already given a recital in Italy, and Eugenia now refers to him as 'Il ffisko'. His training has given his speaking voice a fruity quality and marginally increased his articulacy; he frequently cries 'Gran' dio!' and 'Justi numi!' and babbles in most of the operatic languages. When Fleur Duprat was dining chez ffiske, Cecil burst through the front door and, although he had never met her before, embraced her with a shriek of 'Ma princesse!'

As I turned into Phillimore Gardens on Friday, Il ffisko was on the front doorstep, his genitals in full relief under a pair of spray-on orange shorts; he was off to an erotic encounter in Deptford. Alec appeared in tennis clothes, but he went off to their country seat, looking pained that Eugenia would not accompany him. She and I sat around drinking champagne, the excuse for which was that Friday had been my last day at Simpkin. My eight years there ended with a whimper. Most of the staff are on holiday and so there was no party or presentation of gold watch, though I am to receive an *ex gratia* payment and Old Simpkin has announced a celebration in the autumn. Whether I shall be invited, he did not make clear. The event should not emphasize the finality of my departure, for, in the first place, I shall probably do some odd jobs for S in the time left by the law course and, in the second place, the last time I announced I was leaving for good, I had returned before smoking all the cigars given as a farewell present. On that occasion I was sent off with a drinks party at Topers Cocktail Bar, where we were served a bright green cocktail called Sea Witch, a mixture of Vosene Medicated Shampoo and Dettol. Simpkin drinks parties are always embarrassing, especially if they are held in the shop; the transition from functionary to chirpy conversationalist is too much for the employees, and they all stand pressed to the walls, smiling weakly.

When I left before, it was to work for a Ph.D. at Makreel University, Southern California. The Makreel campus is a hotchpotch of architectural styles, the dominant influence being Cecil B. De Mille; there are several columned imperial monsters with, e.g., 'MVSIC' emblazoned on the pediment. Round the edge are the fraternity and sorority houses called by Greek letters, with loudspeakers playing rock music into the street at full volume. When I arrived in September, the sororities were soliciting for and initiating new members, and frenzied female choruses could be heard screaming the song of their clan and clapping their hands. The centrepoint of the campus is a half-size replica of Big Ben which contains a set of bells; for ten minutes twice every weekday, and for hours on end on Sundays, it chimes out of tune like an ice cream van, massacring the popular classics and playing the role of gentleman from Porlock to the many internationally famous scholars within earshot. The bells are not automatic, but operated by a nonagenarian lady, who climbs hundreds of stairs to reach the levers. In the old days she was restricted by the number of bells to the pentatonic scale, but then a 'benefactor' donated the missing intervals, and the old thing now has chromatic orgies.

The suburban area surrounding the university houses a large number of human relics from the hippie era, who sit on steps with guitars, waist-length hair and headbands. Many of them have had no brain cells since their experiments with narcotics in the sixties, and shuffle about twitching and shouting into dustbins. They were evidently the target of a sign I saw in the local McDonald's, 'No Talking To Invisible People' (a pragmatic fallacy, as one of the local logicians pointed out). The place is also a centre for the physically handicapped; the campus has been specially equipped for them with lifts, ramps and so forth, and they jerk, groan and slaver in whirring hi-tech electric wheelchairs operated by eye movements, whistles or, for the exceptionally able-bodied, switches moved by the hand. A frequent visitor to the Café Greco, on the edge of campus, was a spastic man who could only control his head.

Although speechless, he was a film director and, while I was there, was persuading passing young women (through an interpreter) to take off their clothes and feature in a fantasy movie. I met another spastic who had been at Oxford when I was, and whom I had always avoided in the library in case he asked me to wheel him to the lavatory. The most grotesque sight was a three-foot-long homunculus who went out by himself, lying on a trolley and seeing the way ahead through a series of mirrors. All these people lived at the Center for Independent Living – surely a contradiction in terms.

The philosophy department at Makreel is one of the best in the world. Being lavishly endowed, it buys up eminent philosophers and has recently improved its standing further by hiring several distinguished rats from the sinking British ship. When I arrived the most recent acquisition was the internationally renowned philosopher of science, Stephen Carvell; his seminars were packed, and people stood in the corridor to hear him contradict himself and fumble with objections. I attended a course on ethics by Rodney 'The Thug' Race, a smart aleck with a lecherous face and a repertoire of philosophical examples all involving sports cars and beer. He was followed around by a dumb blonde, whose presence he justified by claiming that she knew about existentialism. Graduate students at American universities are treated like schoolchildren; I had to amass twelve credits by attending lectures, participating in discussions and writing papers, which were graded. The system is more structured than the British one, and if you can tolerate it you end up knowing more about your subject, but the bureaucracy is enervating. I spent the first day of the quarter filling in computer cards, taking a green one to my adviser, who signed it, and then to a professor who changed it for a pink one which I had to take to an official who put an X on it and gave me a purple one which I had to take care not to bend. Entering into the spirit of efficiency, I punched some holes in some of the cards, to store them in a file. Presumably, when fed into the computer, they scrambled the academic and criminal records of all the students in the university.

I was one of five new graduates in the department. The others were a camp German sculptor called Goetz, whose first question to me was whether I was gay; a lugubrious Jew from Ann Arbor; a spiv in clogs, who had taken five years off university to sell advertising space; and a gawky specimen with a repulsive nose, called (the specimen, that is) Lucas Moskovic. Moskovic evidently knew a lot, for his sole method of argument was *ad verecundiam*: he would tell us that we were all wasting our time discussing such-and-such, for we were not addressing the recent advances made in the field by Professors X, Y and Z; then he would recite a list of papers which had been published that week and which apparently we ought to have digested before being entitled to open our mouths. This type – which regards philosophy as a form of technology, in which new results simply replace old – is a menace in seminars. I had independent grounds for disliking Moskovic: he claimed that I looked like my uncle Jake, his former professor. We all met over a weekend organized by the faculty at the Citrus Vale Conference Center, where, as well as mooching on the beach, getting drunk and feeding racoons, we were given advice on how to teach undergraduates. The key, we were told by Professor Chuck Kaase (a sallow man who used to play the saxophone all night in a leather bar), is to 'feign respect' – which made me wonder whether he was only feigning respect for us.

My stipend as Hiram P. Gilbert Fellow (deposited in the local Wells Fargo, where my NatWest traveller's cheques were derided) was enough to let me take a room in the International House, half of whose several hundred residents are American, the other half foreign. The American students who choose to stay there are on the whole back-slapping sports enthusiasts with a limitless toleration of pidgin English, while most of the foreigners are from the Far East and studying applied science. My room was one of fifty matchboxes on a long penitentiary-style corridor. In the box on my right was a mechanical engineer from Korea, in the one on my left a computer scientist from Japan. The Japanese boffin had a nocturnal social life: every night, just after I had put my light out at about 11.30 p.m., there would be a knock on his door, followed by delighted yells of greeting ('*Hazzai!*'); then the television would be turned on and I would lie, tearful with insomnia, until 3.00 a.m., vowing revenge for every decibel that effortlessly penetrated the polystyrene wall. The obvious solutions were unavailing. Complaints met with bafflement and subsequent disregard, ear plugs fell out, and stiff drinks before bed resulted in night-time hikes to the nearest urinal. One night, when it all became too much, I roared an extended 'Shut Up'. There was instant silence, followed a few seconds later by a tiny staccato 'o' from one of the merrymakers. Then the telly went on again and their jabbering resumed at full volume as if nothing had happened.

I-House provided a variety of 'orientation activities' to help us settle in. On Wednesday evenings there was a 'coffee hour', where I met a geotechnical engineer from North Carolina, who for part of his first degree had taken a course in chicken judging: you are given five chickens and trained to predict by, among other things, looking into the whites of their eyes and measuring the distance from breast bone to fanny, which will lay the most eggs. This man also told me how to skin a pig in ten minutes: you plunge it into boiling water (alive or dead?) and the skin comes off in one. In addition he played the mandolin. On our first day we were shown a film called *City of the Angels*, a tourist movie about Los Angeles, from the 'Is it a log? No! It is the deadly croc-o-dile!' stable, which had evidently been shown to the foreign recruits every year since the fifties. The film caused cynical mirth among those whose English was good enough for them to understand it, and bewilderment among the large remainder, one of whom was a depressed Chinese who asked me what 'barbecue' meant. Although foreign graduates entering American universities must pass an examination in English, its standard is that of a picture-book for five-year-olds: 'This is Peter. This is Jane. Here is Peter's ball.' This of course gives rise to problems once the students start work. An African showed me an essay of his, under which the professor had in desperation written, 'Very good. Beta minus.' He could see that his pupil had brains, but the piece was written in three-word sentences.

Among the orientation activities were several outings. The film having whetted my appetite to see Los Angeles, I swallowed my pride and signed up for a coach tour round the city – 'round', as it turned out, in the sense of not entering the city at all but circling it in the suburbs. The bus driver pointed out some 'ancient buildings', a row of late nineteenth century apartment blocks. A more adventurous expedition was the weekend at Moss Boulder Ranch – in season, a summer camp for children. On arrival, the I-House coach-load was shown into a large reception room plastered with posters – some of them bought, some homemade – bearing such messages as 'God will never lead you where his mercy cannot keep you' (in white under two cyclamen flowers), 'Human life is precious, handle with care prayer' and 'Blow on this spot: if it turns red, your teeth need cleaning; if it turns blue, you have a fever; if it stays white, you're well enough to go to church on Sunday' (in fact, previous guests had performed the test so often that the spot had gone grey). The ranch was run by a middle-aged couple, the male of which was of normal height but the shape of a dwarf. His wife gave us a cosy chat in an exaggeratedly kindly voice, telling us that this was their home. 'It's a very large home. Large, but not fancy. The men will be sleeping in huts just up the hill, and the women in huts on the other side. The men's huts have a sign saying "Buoys" [which she pronounced "Booies"] and the women's huts have a sign saying "Gulls". Perhaps you won't understand this if your English isn't very good, but we think it's a lot of fun.' All this was delivered in a style suited to the youngest of her summer residents, and accompanied by wavings of the arm designed, presumably, to explain what she was saying to an international group. The buoys and gulls were then shown to their huts, which turned out each to contain eight beds packed together and to consist on three sides merely of cloth screens of the kind that might be used to keep mosquitoes away. There was no possibility of catching up on lost sleep, for the nights were freezing and nuts kept falling from a tree on to the corrugated-iron roof of my hut.

The weekend finished round a camp fire, where we were joined by the director of I-House, Wilbur Walton, who told us at length how marvellous the House was. Whenever he thought he had said something funny, he would pause, drop his jaw and look slowly round the company, emitting a long, drawling laugh of complicity: Haaaaaaaaaaaaaa. At the end of his speech he invited the different nationalities to sing characteristic songs. Some Indians gave a rendering of 'We Shall Overcome' in Hindi, while I and the other English students managed a rather raucous 'Jerusalem'. My compatriots were unappealing, comprising a wiseacre who kept boasting how he had been thrown out of Stanford for telling the urban planning department it was a dead loss; a former electrician called Ken, whose sophisticated sense of humour revealed itself in the following riddle, 'What's the difference between a goldfish and a wild goat? One mucks about in fountains'; a poetess from Taunton who betrayed herself by carrying around a copy of Lord of the Rings; a former military cadet who, when I told him I was a TA (teaching assistant) in the philosophy department, thought I was in the Territorial Army; and a

Hooray Henry who has since gone into property development. I became friendly, however, with the Chinese who had asked me to explain 'barbecue'. He told me that with my spiky hair I looked Chinese and reminded him of home, and then he brought out pictures of his wife and baby, both of whom seemed to be called Ieuh; he called himself John, but that presumably was to save trouble. We had endless conversations about Oxfor and Cambli, and I did not have the heart to tell him that my name is not Hose.

My orientation was completed by a coach tour of the wine country. I had hoped, as we drove there, to finish the previous night's sleep, but was greeted, as I stumbled on to the coach, by a cry of 'Hose!' and then grilled on the subject of the British aristocracy. We were led around five vineyards, tasting wine at each one and developing a headache. In one of them our guide spoke only Spanish, and his explanation of how to prune a vine was translated for us by a Bolivian mathematician who was among the party. The day ended at the house of a member of the local Rotary Club, where we were entertained round the swimming pool by ancient rotarians. I sat next to an old chap who turned out to be almost stone deaf; at one point I mentioned that the London Library had bought few books since the fifties, to which he replied, 'What! They ain't building ships in Britain any more?' In the distance his wife, squeezed into a pink terylene trouser suit, could be heard saying, 'Ronald Reagan is a wonderful man.'

I should have remained at Makreel for five years, but ran away after six weeks. The proximate cause was insomnia. Of course, if one cannot sleep where one lives, the simplest course is to seek alternative accommodation nearby, and I might have looked for a flat. But all the flats in town were taken, and a garret in a tenement would have been no more soothing than a matchbox in I-House. In any case, lack of sleep had made me irrational, so I decided to put several thousand miles between me and my neighbour. The underlying reason for going is obscure to me; I suspect I was unhappy working in the disciplined framework of exams, grades and regular essays, and that this in turn was due to a fear of being judged. On returning to England I half decided I had made a foolish mistake, and bought another ticket to California. But I repacked my bags in the spirit of a charade, and on the morning I was due to leave I unpacked them again for good.

The vacillation had turned me into a nervous wreck, so to cheer me up my mother took me to Battersea Dog's Home to look for a replacement for our old cat Sausage, who had recently died in his twentieth year. He had become very doddery and was barely able to climb the stairs; a friend unkindly claimed that he had been dead for years and that we merely moved the corpse about the house from time to time. When we took Sausage to the vet for an enema, my mother asked the latter whether he thought S had lost a tooth. 'Let's put it this way: he's *got* a tooth,' the man replied. I turned against him for this callous quip; in any case he was obviously incompetent with animals, for he had only nine fingers left. Over Christmas Sausage's condition worsened, and the Old Dear and I raised the question of euthanasia. Sausage must have lip-read our discussion (he had been deaf for some time) as, on the day we had planned to have him finished off, he keeled over while eating his breakfast. He was still breathing while the OD carried him up to her bed, and he passed away peacefully on the eiderdown as she stroked him. I dug a grave at the corner of our field – strenuous work, this, as the ground was water-logged and groined with roots. Returning to the house, I found Sausage curled up, as if asleep, in a patch of his own pee. *Rigor mortis* had set in, so when I picked him up he remained curled in a ball. The funeral procession (the OD, the corpse and I) set off for the field, trying to keep out of view of Bird's house, as Mrs Bird was at this time upstairs dying of cancer and might have taken the event as an omen. When we reached the grave, it had filled with water. Sausage eddied in circles as I threw earth on top of him and the OD wiped away a tear. The following year we planted a rose over the spot – I was nervous that an ear might appear when I was preparing the ground – but this was later consumed when Willy Prike, who is supposed to keep the field tidy, burned the grass instead of mowing it. As a result of this desecration, the exact site of Sausage's remains is now unknown.

9 September

Last week the Old Dear was in Venice with Clarence and Peggy Butt. I had feared – and so, I imagine, had she – that she would be nostalgic and depressed, comparing her package holiday with the grand trips she made with my father (they used to stay at the Hotel Regina in a room with a large balcony looking across the Grand Canal to San Salute). But she came back saying she was glad she had gone, despite the prickly C. Butt's floating querulousness, which hooks itself on to anything he can manage to be irritated by. It is surprising how good-humoured Peggy has remained after thirty-nine years with this pain in the neck.

I was left cat-sitting and, to avoid lavatory attendant's duties on the balcony at Basil Mansions, took the Little Dears to the country, where they tormented smaller animals and I read The Countess of Pembroke's Arcadia. Rackman had mortified me by revealing that he had read both Arcadia and The Faerie Queene, so I was compelled to buy a yard of Elizabethan literature. He might have mentioned how boring Arcadia is. The Old Dear does not like being at Frogs Cottage by herself, as she is frightened of possible violent burglars and mad axemen. I am frightened of Edie. One evening as I was making supper, E's death's-head of a face loomed up at the kitchen window, making me drop a pan of Bolognese in terror. She claimed that she was looking for Lupin, who had got out – which I knew to be rubbish, as the one skill left to Edie in her senility is that of keeping the poor animal imprisoned in her bungalow. I curtly promised to look for him after dinner but, by the time I had eaten, all Edie's lights were out and she was presumably in bed with Lupin lying across her knees.

Abram endeared himself to me on my return to London by taking me to a Japanese restaurant – his way of letting me know that he had been given a raise. Judging by his expression when the bill came, it was a generous gesture. Not having booked, we were instructed by the head waiter to leave by 9.00 p.m., which was made difficult by our ordering a set meal of many courses. We gobbled away while a backlog of dishes, delivered by waitresses who looked nervously at their watches, piled up around us. Abram then tottered flatulently off to his lover, a painter called Samantha Salisbury-Loake, who lives in Battersea with her thirteen-year-old son Theodore. 'I hope Theodore's in bed,' Abram mumbled forebodingly.

The following morning I delivered to the Empire Road Palazzo a standing lamp, a folding table and a rug, which I had found in the shed at Frogs Cottage. Rackman greeted them ungraciously, fearing that such chattels would give me a right of permanent occupancy. He was particularly sour about the rug because it was dusty and had a dead moth on it. R is currently looking for a new char lady, the old one – a four-foot high Singhalese with one eye – having found the conditions intolerable. An advertisement has been put in the local paper and a questionnaire left by the phone to be presented to the applicants as they ring up. Rackman has something against the Irish and people from Chad, so one of the questions, which cannot be posed directly, concerns ethnic origin. I am put to such shifts as asking the woman her name and then saying, 'Zora. That's an unusual name. Where is it from?'

Fortunately most of the calls have been taken by the new lodger Joanne (or, as she pronounces it in her caricature of an Australian accent, Jow-enn), who is twenty-five and absurdly thin. I, renowned as a drink of water, have womanly curves in comparison; judging by her hips, childbearing is out of the question. Jow-enn is bright with a passive sense of humour, giggling at everything I say and even at some things Rackman says, and is suspiciously helpful with the washing up – a ploy of upmanship which perhaps will be dropped when it has established her in our minds as a good type. She is highly strung, talking to herself and taking a hot water bottle to bed in the summer. Underwear and personal hygiene are painful subjects to her: she refuses to hang her washing in the utility room, fearing that Rackman, Leslie and I will examine her knickers, and prefers to put out a line in the garden, which for obscure reasons she thinks more discreet. On arriving she insisted that a lock be fitted to the door of the bathroom, and now spends whole mornings pottering about in there. If she wants to go to the lavatory but thinks it is occupied, she is too timid to try the door and instead traipses round the house to establish the whereabouts of the other residents. If one is missing, she deduces that he is at stool – an unsafe inference, as she discovered the other morning: after half an hour's increasing discomfort, she braved the risk of seeing a man with his trousers down, opened the door, found the lavatory empty and realized that Rackman, who she had thought was in there reading Henry James, had left for the office. These are symptoms of the artistic temperament. She has told Rackman that she intends to be a world-famous pianist, but clearly she is too old and is receiving an unsuitable training; neither Maurizio Pollini nor Radu Lupu studied at the Peckham Conservatoire and received lessons from a fellow-national in Dulwich. It is unlikely that we shall have a chance to assess her artistry as, thank God, she is not bringing the threatened piano.

On Saturday evening I entertained Dick Randall, his wife Suzanne and a political theorist called Chris Dalton whom I had got to know at Makreel. Dalton's most recent post was as fifty per cent of the personnel in the politics department at the American University in Cairo. A few months after he went to Egypt I received a card from him postmarked Berlin, where he had fled. Cairo had proved intolerable: on arrival he was bitten by a mad dog, soon afterwards his stomach succumbed to Egyptian cuisine, and the yelling of the muezzin – who nowadays use loud-hailers – gave him insomnia. In a triumph of hope over experience, he is going to teach next spring in Brazil, where he will have to teach in Portuguese. So far he knows four words. I was able to add a fifth, 'ovos', meaning eggs. I learned it on holiday in the Algarve with my parents. Going to the village shop, we tried to buy some eggs by referring to them in all the languages we knew, which did not include Portuguese. Each time we were met with open-mouthed bafflement from the old lady behind the counter. In desperation my father drew the outline of a chicken, with a schematic leg and a dotted line running from its bottom to an egg. The lady was equally puzzled by this and, when eventually she grasped what we wanted, she managed to convey that she had thought it was a drawing of a one-legged chicken doing peepee. Dick Randall, a friend from school, is largely responsible for my having wasted twelve years doing philosophy. When I was about fifteen I saw a copy of Russell's *History* on his desk and decided that I could not allow him the superiority of having read it when I had not. Then the rot set in. Dick is like Robert Robinson, with less sparkle, and works as a publisher. His wife spent much of the evening, to D's annoyance and mine, going on about Abram's sexiness, which she attributed to his half-closed eyes. These are in fact explained by his being myopic and too vain to wear spectacles; he can often be seen walking in a haze down St James's, ignoring old friends and greeting strangers.

On Monday evening I was reunited with Ellénore, who had returned, looking like a Schwarze, from a six-week holiday in Spain, where she has, as she puts it, a 'home'. After a Marks and Spencer dinner, we had a night of passion followed by a day of passion, interrupted only by a visiting plumber. While he was upside-down under the immersion heater, E made me open a bottle of champagne and, when he righted himself and saw us drinking it, he gave us a people-like-you-make-me-puke look. He would have been pleased by our headaches a couple of hours later. Mine interfered with a shopping expedition to Lena's to buy ravioli to give Moses and Judy for supper. Moses, not realizing that eight of Lena's ravioli are like two Shredded Wheat, attempted twelve and ended the evening in dyspeptic silence. Before that, however, he declared, as usual, that all women should be beaten to death and, as he swallowed his tenth raviolo, he managed to gasp that, since hardly anyone is worth educating, all universities but one should be closed. Jow-enn, not having met the little fellow before, was amazed that anyone should assert such a view; he, irritated by her sanity, pushed his claim further, ending at the position that only one person needs to be educated at a time, to be the next philosopher-king. Meanwhile Judy, depressed by her job at an Indian travel agent's, quietly poured bottle after bottle of Rioja down her throat and ended by lusting tearfully after a sponge cake that Rackman had confected and that was standing on the sideboard. Rackman eats his cakes with cream for breakfast and, as there was only one half-pound wedge left, it would have been more than my life is worth to let her loose on it. This cake in particular was a sore subject with my landlord, for as soon as it had come out of the oven he

90

kindly traipsed to the top of the house with a modest sliver for Leslie. 'What do you think?' Rackman asked smugly. 'Doesn't travel well,' Leslie replied, damning himself for good.

19 September

I am now enrolled at NIPLES and pursuing a leisurely course of study. The day begins at 3.00 p.m., we are given two lectures and at 5.00 p.m. we all go home. I feel this will not last. No written work has been set, though the lecturers have recommended textbooks, which I am reading with enjoyment. The law is congenial to the logic-chopping mind, and some of the problems in criminal law take me back to my youthful studies in the philosophy of action. (A sets off to kill B. While driving to B's house, he runs over a man who turns out to be B. Why isn't A guilty of murder?) I have learned various interesting facts, such as that in certain circumstances shaking your fist can make you guilty of assault. Some of the cases are engaging: I have come across one involving a slug in a ginger-beer bottle and another in which a man makes a woman nervously ill by telling her, for a practical joke, to go with two cushions to pick up her husband who is lying outside a pub in Leytonstone with both his legs broken. The trouble is that I cannot remember either what the cases are called (the latter I think of as the Leytonstone Legs Case) or what they establish. Memory, I suspect, will be a problem; the textbooks are huge and, although they pose no serious intellectual difficulties to one of my prodigious analytic power, the thought that by next summer their contents must be inside my head is dispiriting. In philosophy you need to think a lot and know little; in law it is the other way round.

The lectures take place in a faceless building off the Gray's Inn Road. It is not encouraging to the student to reflect why anyone would want to give lectures in a professional solicitors' course. If the lecturer knows his subject, he could be earning five times as much in practice, while if he is academically gifted he would be happier in a university, so there is a case for thinking that all the NIPLES's lecturers are bad lawyers. In fact they seem competent, despite their irritating features: Mr Taylor (Constitutional) adopts a yo-ho-ho manner and puts on silly accents; Mr Lees (Contract) has a tedious bleating voice and strings together clichés about pigs in pokes, throwing good money after bad, people's being worth powder and shot, and having the readies; Mr Bennett (Trusts) looks like a member of the IRA and has only one hand, rolling up the sleeve of his truncated arm and waving the stump around in a fight against embarrassment; Mrs Erasmus (Land) dictates at a speed guaranteeing cramp and illegibility; and Mr Hackett (Tort) is an old buffer from the pages of Dickens, who publicly humiliates latecomers. The class contains about thirty-five students, more than half of them women, more than half of these attractive. One has the most voluptuous mouth I have seen, which she pursed in irritation when she caught me leering at her, and there is a beautiful token black who is called Laetitia but says she prefers to be called Ndombu (*chacun à son gout*). None of us has studied law before, and the majority are arts graduates. I have however met an expert in acid rain, and asked him whether it was true – as Abram told me – that farting repairs the damage done to the ozone layer by aerosols. He said this was a simplistic theory.

Furthering an aspiration to Renaissance manhood, I have also enrolled on a Latin course at the City Lit. The red tape this involves will deter any but the most resolute self-improver. You arrive in the morning to pick up a ticket that will admit you in the evening, which you spend standing in queues next to Trotskyists who are signing up for classes in mime or self-assertion-for-women. By the time I reached the fifth queue, I was expecting a number to be stamped on my wrist. Having been told to go away until I was called, I went to the canteen, where sausage and chips had just stopped being served, then to the bar, where I was jeered at for drinking Bourbon by two youths with blue hair, and ended up sitting in the Institute's theatre, trying to concentrate on *Arcadia* while students were auditioning for the drama course. Lesson one begins on the 22nd; the reader is referred to the next instalment for details.

After a sybaritic weekend chez Ellénore, I went to see Rebecca on Sunday evening. When she asked me why I had not received a phone message left at Empire Road that morning, I heard myself telling her about my affair with E – a revelation I had been half-intending to make for some time. I assumed it would be of only academic interest to Rebecca, for, when she came for the weekend two months ago, she said there was no future in her own relationship with me, and since then has seldom been in touch. However, she became indignant and accused me of jumping to unwarranted conclusions as a result of my refusal ever to 'talk things through'. 'If I had wanted us to stop being lovers,' she said, 'I wouldn't have left you to infer it. I would have told you.' I replied that the move from 'She told me there was no future in our relationship' to 'She does not want us to continue being lovers' barely deserved the title of an inference; but R replied that I was only meant to take her remark as a request for us to Talk Things Through. That is, I was meant, not to take the remark literally, but to draw an inference from it. There is an inconsistency here which I was too irritated to unravel. When I asked why, if she wanted our affair to continue, she had made so little effort to see me, she made a flimsy excuse about being busy at the office and having problems with her flat. Now she is under less pressure, she would like to turn me on again like the radio – except that she is just off for a three-week holiday in America. For disregarding this purely nominal

93

association, I am in her eyes a cad. She showed no signs of wanting to provide the dinner she had invited me for, so I set off across London for a pork pie at home. Rebecca is not one to overlook an excuse for self-righteousness, and is doubtless now blackening my reputation among our common friends. I asked her to send me a card from the States to show she was still a chum, but she looked unenthusiastic.

On Monday I had lunch with uncle Jake, a famous philosopher who has spent most of his eighty years in Canada. Jake is one of those men who are eminent without ever having done anything much. He has written some workmanlike philosophy books and edited some others, but he is no more clever or profound than hundreds of other contemporary philosophers; nevertheless he is found in every index and every undergraduate has heard of him. Jake is widely and justly recognized to be the nastiest man in philosophy – not an easy title to earn – and is boundlessly conceited. He is uninterested in conversation but likes to soliloquize to an audience about his merits. Thus he once said to me, 'I've just written a paper called [so-and-so]. I think the title is so good, I don't know why I bothered to write the paper.' On another occasion he recalled how he had been invited to give a lecture and the chairman introduced him with a rapturous eulogy; 'When he had finished,' Jake said, 'I stood up and said "After hearing that introduction, I can't wait to hear what I'm going to say." ' He also likes to recall how he worsted such-and-such a notable philosopher at a conference. I saw him exercise this skill when he delivered some lectures in London a few years ago. Having outlined a definition of universalizability, he said, 'So much, I think, is uncontroversial. But, if anyone wanted to object to my assumptions, this would be the place to do so.' This clearly was not an invitation, but the aged Professor Rosemary Seale, an old enemy of Jake's, started raising an objection from the back of the

94

hall. Having shut her up peremptorily, Jake continued and later, to illustrate a point, said, 'If, for instance, someone gratuitously interrupted a lecture. . .' A clattering was heard on the back row, and Seale was seen waddling out. Believing himself to be one of the world's great philosophers, Jake is contemptuous of those who are more generally agreed to be the leading thinkers, but he is generous towards second-rankers, who he thinks are so far beneath him that he can afford to be indulgent. He has never encouraged his nephew's philosophical efforts, and was savagely rude about a paper I showed him when I was an undergraduate. He gave me a paper of his in return, which I threw into the dustbin as I left his hotel. Jake is also mean about money. He will seldom pay for a meal and, if he knows someone else is paying, will order the most expensive dish. Once my parents took him and the late auntie Leah out to dinner. My father asked him if he would like a brandy and he declined, but, when my mother's brandy was brought, Jake leaned over the table and appropriated it.

Jake was in London on Monday on his way to Cambridge, where he spends every other winter as a fellow of St Luke's College. This is less of an honour than it seems, for visiting fellows at St Luke's invite themselves and pay for board and lodging. In London he was staying at the In and Out Club – an unsuitably military residence for a philosopher, but the club has some link with his university. Jake now has a stroke behind him, and he tottered towards me across the lobby at half a mile an hour. He has a generous provision of an old man's disgusting habits, knocking his food all over the table, choking in mid-sentence and letting his nose run into the soup. As usual he burbled on about himself, recounting how he fell down a flight of granite steps in Vienna and putting me off my tucker by displaying the scar on the top of his head. (The old boy should not be let out without a nurse; when he was last in London he managed to plunge down some steps into somebody's area.) I sat like a nana with a smile fixed to my face, nodding and saying yes occasionally and wishing I were dining with the man at the next table – a pinguid colonel with a purple face and an enraged expression, who was washing some beef down with a great deal of beer. The system of payment at the In and Out is such that Jake was forced to sign for the lunch himself, but he made me pay for coffee in the smoking-room, pretending he had no change. As I left he said, 'Give my regards to your mother. It's been far too long since we met.' When I repeated this to the Old Dear, she retorted, 'It hasn't been long enough.'

Jake was the eldest of four siblings. My father Saul was two years younger, then came uncle Felix, and lastly auntie Carmel, who was an artist and died nearly twenty years ago. Felix, the only other survivor, lives in Colindale (end of Northern Line) and is a semi-retired PR man – proof that you don't need charm to succeed in public relations. We hear from him only when he is somewhere exotic, for then he will send a card to let us know what an interesting life he leads. The cards are usually laconic; the last said, 'Greetings from Caracas. Felix.' He and auntie Maureen produced two children, Jane and Clive. Jane married a dwarf from Giggleswick and I imagine Clive went to the bad, for when he was a small boy Felix and Maureen used to decry him to his face. 'Of course, Clive is a complete idiot,' they would say, as the little chap looked gloomily at the floor. Felix courted Maureen while they shared a tandem, and they were contentedly married till her death forty years later. On that occasion my mother received a photo-copied threnody from Felix, which lamented Maureen by stating how useful she had been in his PR business, now employing X people with a turnover of Y pounds, opening a new office in Z, and so on. Auntie Maw's funeral bak'd meats did coldly furnish forth the tables at Felix's marriage to one Rene, who lived across the road and had presumably been waiting for years.

Jake, Saul, Felix and Carmel were the children of a book-keeper from Odessa, the Birkenhead of the Black Sea. (My maternal grandfather was a mechanical engineer from the Birkenhead of the Mersey.) In 1912 Grandpa North – Poops, as he was known – brought his wife (Moomps) and two infant sons (Felix and Carmel were not yet born) to England. The reason for the move is obscure; one explanation is that there was widespread antisemitism in Russia at the time and the family was Jewish. (I have the worst of both worlds: not having a Jewish mother, I am excluded from Seder nights, but, with a Jewish father, I would have a star sewn on me in a Nazi uprising.) Poops had no friends here and knew not a word of English, but he managed to establish himself in Hackney, running tin-pot businesses and publishing 'North's Directory' – a forerunner of the Yellow Pages for North East London. The family's income was eked out by lodgers, but Poops was an unreliable landlord. One day he met a man who for a hobby painted feathers – not pictures of feathers: he applied paint to the feathers themselves. (Remember the domestic tragedies that resulted a few years ago when *Blue Peter* ran a Paint Your Dog competition.) Poops was thunderstruck by the feathers' beauty. 'You must leave your job!' he cried to the man. 'Come and live with us, and you can devote yourself to your art. You will make a fortune!' The man handed in his notice and moved in, but his genius remained unrecognized. Soon Poops tired of his non-paying guest and kicked him out. The man was left jobless, homeless and penniless. Poops was always keen to improve his properties. On one occasion he decided it would be nice to have a cellar, so he pulled up the carpet in the front room and started digging. Each time he emerged from the hole, he looked more worried, but Moomps could not persuade him to tell her what was the matter. Finally he had to admit that he had reached the water-table; the hole was filling up and threatening to flood the house.

97

At the outbreak of the First World War Poops decided to seek his fortune in America, and set off, leaving Moomps and the children (there were now four) to survive on the rents from tenants. Life was hard, and it may have been at this time that Moomps developed the technique of boiling a chicken for its stock and then serving the dehydrated bird for dinner. Tension in the home was increased by the fact that Saul, who was hopeless at school, had a mortal hatred of Jake, who was always top of the class. Moomps came home from shopping one day to find Saul chasing Jake round the dining-room table with a carving knife, screaming, 'I'll kill you, I'll kill you!' If he had succeeded, the world would have been deprived of a *Commentary on Hegel's Logic*, a refutation of sense-datum theory and a defence of prescriptivism. Poops's years in the USA were spent in the movies; he was not an actor or member of a film crew, but, finding nothing to do, used to spend all day sitting in the cinema. He returned to England at the end of the war and managed, on the day before the armistice was declared, to join the Russian army. For some time afterwards he could be seen strutting around Hackney in Russian uniform. This seems to have been part of an access of nostalgia for the old country, for at this time he also converted all his money into roubles, believing that their value would soar under the new Bolshevik regime. The converse happened and he was ruined.

Poops's sense of humour was mischievous. For years he had hated the rabbi Perlsveig's moustache, so, when the Norths and the Perlsveigs went to Brighton for the day, he waited for the rabbi to fall asleep on the beach and then shaved off half the moustache. But he was gentle to the point of squeamishness. Hours would be spent putting flies out of the window without hurting them, and Poops refused to attend the ceremony of my circumcision. 'I can't bear to hear the little chap scream,' he said to my mother, and sat with her in a neighbouring room in the maternity hospital, wincing at every baby's cry he heard. After the circumcision the moil came into the room and said 'Maseltof' to my mother. 'Maseltof to you too,' she replied, not knowing what it meant.

Poops was contemptuous of women. When my mother offered to drive him round the block in her new car, he refused with horror, and he repeatedly said of Moomps that she was 'rotten to the core'. Moomps was in fact a battle-axe. After Poops died, she continued to live in 6 Balthazar Road with a companion called Sonia, whom she called a servant and whom she treated in the way a Tsarina would treat a serf. 'Clean the floor, Sonia!' she would bark peremptorily, and, when the poor old thing had done so, would toss her a sixpence. These occasional gratuities were Sonia's only income. Sonia was a kind lady who was fond of children and, when my parents and I used to visit on Sundays, she would take me into the back garden to pat next door's dog over the wall. The sit-down Sunday teas – at which the cups of tea were served with hot milk – were dreary affairs and became increasingly so as Moomps lapsed into senility. 'Vere are ze children?' she would ask, not realizing that one of them, my father, was sitting there, middle-aged and hence unrecognized. After tea I would watch *Fireball XL5* on the telly, my mother would knit in self-defence and Moomps would try and foist oranges on us. 'Hev an orange!' 'No thank you, we've just had tea.' 'Vy not? Zeyre perfectly good oranges!' (My father's eccentric English – he would say 'pillow box' for 'pillar box' and, in the manner of a sixteenth century madrigal, 'besides' for 'beside' – is explained by the fact that he learned it at Moomps's knee.) As we left, she would always stand on the doorstep and call, 'Don't forget 6 Balthazar!'

When Moomps was very gaga she came to stay in our flat, under the impression that she was at a hotel in Eastbourne. One afternoon my mother took her to sit in Hereford Square. 'Send for some tea,' Moomps commanded. 'You can't get tea here,' my mother snapped, and then, to her dismay, caught sight of a tea tray being brought out by a resident of one of the houses on the square. 'Let's go home for tea,' she suggested, hustling Moomps away. 'Oh no,' said Moomps, 'zey serve a horrid cup of tea in dat hotel.' She was a trial, frightening me and getting under the feet of our maid Enid, to whom she threw the odd bit of change as she had done to Sonia. My parents used to sneak into her bedroom when she was asleep, and put the alarm clock back three hours to keep her out of the way in the morning. She ended up in an old people's home, terrorizing the inmates.

27 September

Sandra Morrison – composer and old friend of the family – came to lunch at Frogs Cottage last Sunday with a view to seeing Edie. The previous time Sandra came to a meal, she choked on a French bean and, to the surprise of the other guests, threw up the contents of her oesophagus over the dinner table. This time she was given an easy-to-swallow cauliflower with her roast beef, and the lunch passed without incident. To have had Edie at the table would have resulted in our passing round the carving knife to slit our wrists, so S went round to visit her afterwards. Edie greeted Sandra, whom she has known for half a century, with the 'How good of you to drop in' that she addresses to people she is not sure whether she has met before, and, when S had gone, asked my mother, 'Have you ever met Sandra Morrison?' She also recently asked the Old Dear whether she had ever met Saul North. 'I was married to him for over twenty years,' the OD replied. 'Really?' gasped Edie, 'no-one ever told me.'

On Tuesday evening I had my first Latin lesson at the City Lit. There was a timetable in the entrance hall showing where the various classes were being held, and a commissionaire to help anyone not bright enough to read it. The Commissionaire was himself dyslexic, but also officious. Having seen that the Latin Rapid Foundation Course was in room twenty-nine, I was setting off up the stairs when he caught my arm and insisted on finding the class on the notice; it took me some time to explain to him where it was. Room twenty-nine would have comfortably held a seminar of six, but thirty-five students turned up and the class began like that scene in *A Night at the Opera*. Most of them were absolute tyros and at least half had at best a nodding acquaintance with the methods of formal education. There was an old trout who could never find the right page, and an unbalanced black woman, with only one lens in her spectacles, who would raise truculent and irrelevant objections. Unsurprisingly, the 'rapid' course moved at a geological pace, most of the one and a half hours being spent on the conjugation of 'sum'. The teacher, a competent and pleasant woman who speaks Latin with a North Country accent, told me I could move up a level, which I may do, for although I wanted to begin at the beginning, I do not want to remain there. Even Level Three (Intermediate) does not seem awesomely highbrow: the pupils there are now on the perfect tense, having presumably taken two years to reach it.

Ellénore graciously offered to cook dinner for some of my friends, so on Wednesday I vicariously entertained Abram and his newish lover Samantha at E's flat. I had first met Samantha the week before, when she did the same for Abram. She is a divorcee of forty, short and wizened (her claim is unbelievable that she once weighed eleven stone as a result of eating *Sachertorte* over a long period), and has a mouth that turns up at the corners like a cat's. Her implausibly red hair is so tightly permed that it looks like a crash helmet, and the blotches of purple makeup on her cheekbones would qualify her as an Avon lady. She was friendly and nervously garrulous, displaying her erudition excessively, as in a pointless pun on 'Albertus Magnus'; in this, as in some aspects of her appearance, she reminded me of Abram's old flame Libby. Abram had obviously given me a good press in advance, and I was ashamed to think how I never let an opportunity pass to malign him for the sake of a laugh. Ellénore's dinner was predictably elaborate; we ate gravlax, followed by an Indian dish of lamb coated in an exquisite sludge of garlic and almonds, and ended, in the manner of the finest Berni Inns, with Irish coffee served in glasses which had the words 'Irish Coffee' on them. By this time Abram had lapsed into silence, as he was succumbing to a bug that by the following morning had left both him and Ellénore vomiting and feverish. A case could be made that the dinner had poisoned them, but, since the other fifty per cent of the diners remained in radiant health, it would have to be assumed that the salmonellae had confined themselves to one end of the joint of meat.

I learned of Abram's decline when I went to Samantha's flat again on Thursday evening, this time for a drinks party. Clearly this was a gathering of the intelligentsia, since everyone but me appeared to have written a book and to be a friend of Freddy Ayer's. I was introduced to an eminent-looking Greek, whose name I could not remember but was sure I should have heard of, and to an aged journalist whose snuff-taking habits Abram had warned me about. Contrary to expectation, his shirt was not covered in powder, but he did have a Hitler moustache of brown mucus that oozed from his nostrils between sniffs. The food consisted of fried patties and mouth-sized pieces of pizza, which the guests nibbled before going on to the Etoile or the White Tower; but I, being unwaged, treated them as dinner and helped myself to as many as I could each time they were handed round, to the increasing mirth of the waitress. This resulted in a queasy night.

3 October

The Old Dear, who has not met Ellénore, has shown
disapproval of our affair ('Too old,' she snapped), so I
pretended that my visit to E at the end of last week –
which prevented the OD and me from going to the country
till Saturday morning – was a party at NIPLES. (The
party in fact took place yesterday; v. *infra*.) Since we
only arrived at lunchtime, the OD could not give Edie her
breakfast, and was frightened that Bird, who was bound
to have stepped in, would be aggrieved. No sooner had
we stepped through the door than Edie appeared to see
where her lunch was, on the pretext – as always – that
she was wondering whether she could borrow a tin of
Whiskas for Lupin. E totters across so often that we
keep the doors locked and hide behind the curtains
when we see her coming; I recently caught the OD kneel-
ing on the landing and peering over the stairhead to
make sure the coast was clear. Edie's neighbours keep
her fridge groaning with food for the cat. The OD recently
pointed to a tin and cried in exasperation, 'What's that,
Edie?' 'A tin.' 'And what's that a picture of, on the
label?' 'A cat.' 'There you are then, *cat food!*' the OD
shouted, her teeth clenched. 'Would you give him some?'
quavered Edie. 'You give him some, he's your cat!' 'As a
matter of fact, he's not my cat.' 'Whose is he, then?' the
OD asked in amazement. 'He's yours,' Edie replied. The
OD counted to eighty. 'Very well then,' she said briskly,
'if he's mine, I'm going to let him out for some air. You've
kept the poor animal shut up in here for over a year.' But
Edie pleaded with her not to let Lupin out, and she
relented. In fact, Bird told us that Lupin did manage to
escape last week, but he was so nonplussed by freedom
that he just sat down behind the standpipe and let his
drooling mistress scoop him into her arms. He may also
have been weakened by unsuitable diet; when the OD
visited Edie on Sunday, she found that E had given Lupin
a dish of sliced banana with his saucer of milk. During

that visit Edie said to the OD, 'I've got something to tell you. I've decided to make my home here.' Since she has lived in that bungalow for the past fourteen years, this was hardly news; perhaps it was a garbled expression of a fear of being put in an old people's home.

Transistor, having set off for a holiday in Italy, invited her old flame Jurgen – the lugubrious youth with faltering English and Schwarzenegger physique (v. 12 June) – to stay at the Empire Road Mausoleum and, when I returned on Sunday evening, I found that Rackman had installed the tedious beefcake in my bedroom. Seeing my lips purse and my knuckles whiten on the door handle, R suggested ironically that I join him, Jurgen and Stella for dinner. Stella was at Oxford with R and me, and R has been in love with her ever since. He proposed to her three times, and each time she said, 'Don't be silly.' An acceptance would have been disastrous for Rackman, or anyone else; for Stella, while physically desirable to those who are attracted by Edith Piaf, is a bundle of neuroses, visiting an analyst four times a week (at 7.00 a.m. for a reduced charge) and whining about life in general, and men in particular. She is eristically argumentative and can usually catch her interlocutor out on some verbal trifle. Recently an act of God enabled her to confute even Abram, another admirer of old. As usual she was going on about how everyone seemed to be persecuting her, and, as they were crossing Regent Street, Abram said, 'I never feel people are out to get me.' At that moment a sports car roared past, missing A by an inch. 'We'll get you next time!' the passenger shouted.

Stella has a house in Corunna Road, Finsbury Park, which she fills with lodgers in the same way as Rackman. I lived in it briefly after running away from America, but soon ran away from there as well. S terrorized me and the other lodger, Herb, an amiable graduate in English from Cambridge who spent the day reading science fiction comics (his favourite character was Chemo the Laser Man). I was so uncomfortable in Corunna Road that I had frequent dreams about defecating in public places. The last nail in the coffin of my self-respect was a dispute over a dustbin. Stella had been wondering what the neighbours would think about the rusty and lidless piece of scrap metal in the front garden and said that, if I would buy a new bin from the caterers' ironmongers round the corner from Simpkin, she would pay me for it. Ingratiatingly, I brought home in a taxi a sleek black rubber work of art, but, although I never mentioned the fare, my landlady made a scene over the price of the bin and refused to pay. A few days later I slunk off to the Old Dear's.

Finsbury Park (which, spelled backwards, is Krap y rub snif) is more exotic than Catford. The house next door belonged to a family of Azerbaijanis, and the ladies would sit on the front step smoking a hookah between them and looking as if they had walked out of the picture on the Balkan Sobranie tin. The ground floor flat of Stella's house was occupied by a man with a wooden leg, and one used to see odd numbers of socks on his washing line. He would also hang his budgie on the line (in its cage). Across the road was a disorderly house; I was awoken one night by a dissatisfied client shouting, 'I'll kill the cunt!' The area is well known for prostitution at down-to-earth prices, and I was once, when coming home from work, used as a guineapig in a pimp's lesson to a new employee. As I turned down Corunna Road there was a woman standing on the pavement about twenty yards ahead, and a man a bit further on. When I approached her, he said in a kindly voice, 'Come on, darlin',' apparently telling her to hurry up. She then put her hand on my arm and said, with identical intonation, 'Come on, darlin'.' I walked on impassively and he hurried up to her, saying 'No, no, no' in irritation. The most striking sight I saw was a tall woman with peroxide hair,

105

mincing down the Blackstock Road in stilettoes and a leather mini skirt, with no arms.

I told Jow-enn how I had excluded Leslie from a dinner party and how he had sat eating sardines in the kitchen. She had thought this unpardonably cruel. But on Sunday evening Rackman, despite my mild remonstrations, gave her the Leslie treatment, and she has barely spoken to either of us since. I had eaten a large lunch of roast chicken, but managed to force down three helpings of the chicken R had roasted for dinner, as well as some kipper pâté on toast, two bowls of thick soup prepared by Jurgen and three helpings of rice pudding. After the meal we all lay on the dining room floor and gasped. J invited R and me out to dinner on either Monday or Tuesday, but I found an excuse for each evening – the one for Monday being that I had to work. In fact I spent the evening sitting about and eating chocolate biscuits while J was in the house; I hope he thought I looked busy. On Tuesday evening I had my second Latin lesson – and the last. Having sacrificed two tickets for *The Pearl Fishers* (they went to the Old Dear, who took a girl from her tap dancing class and told me afterwards that the opera was about a lot of men wearing nappies), I spent an hour and a half grinding my teeth and drumming the table while the teacher moved at a pace that would have tried the patience of a mentally retarded dyslexic with severe sensory impairment. As she went round the class, making each of us conjugate 'habito', she asked us our names; there was an uncomfortable moment when a man announced himself as Peter and she misheard it as Freda. Despite the ludicrously leisurely speed, she would stop frequently and say, 'Has everyone followed so far?' 'I'm afraid I'm completely at sea,' an old girl moaned from the back, 'I don't know why I can't grasp it.' Bubbles came out of the heads of everyone else, containing the words, 'Because you are a moron.' I think I shall try teaching myself from the textbook; I have become friendly with a classicist called Sandy who is on the law course and who – since I lent him some notes – might help me with problems. Sandy applied for articles at a firm in Streatham and, on his way to an interview there, decided to cut across Tooting Common. He had not remembered that the common was bisected by a railway line and ended up clambering over embankments in his Sunday suit and risking electrocution.

My fear of being the oldest student at NIPLES is unrealized, for there is also a mother of two teenage children, a man with nine years' experience in the Hong Kong Police (given the HKP's reputation for machismo, he looks rather willowy, but perhaps packs a good rabbit-punch), an appalling feminist of mature years who asks fatuous questions during lectures to show that she is uninhibited, and a large, loud and merry lady of thirty-eight called Shirley, who for the past thirteen years has been a university lecturer in anthropology and shouts in a Mancunian brogue. Unfortunately Shirley equally prevents the realization of my desire to be the only doctor on the course; the acid rain man has handed in a Ph.D. thesis on simple radicals, whatever they are, but has not yet been examined. Only a small proportion of the students seem to have started the course straight after their first degree, though there is an irritating cabal of giggly girls who appear not to have seen much of life and look as if they would be more at home in a typing pool. Among the other old timers I have met a former diamond-setter and a pyknic figure whose career so far has embraced lorry driving, membership of a punk band and a job with British Telecom. We are gradually getting to know each other through brief conversations before lectures. The decibel level the lecturer must overcome to attract attention grows daily: law students are more garrulous and gregarious than philosophy students, who await their lectures in silence, wrapped in Angst and Cartesian doubt. Friday evening was the first formal occasion for getting acquainted, when the Institute laid on drinks in an upstairs room at the Nag's Head; the alcohol apart, it was a setting suitable for a nineteenth century Methodist meeting. I spent some time talking to Mr Bennett, the lecturer with the eloquent stump, who confirmed the theory that city law firms are sweatshops. I said I was worried that I would not have time at Savage Borman to pursue my other interests, and he replied that I need not worry, for I would find that I soon lost all my other interests. We also had a meeting this week with some students in their second year. They all agreed that there was no point reading the textbooks, which depressed me, since I am now 300 pages into four out of the six I have bought and, like Macbeth, am too far in to go back. I have also been checking some of the cases in the casebooks and have been numbed by the prolixity of most judges: having made their point, the old boys then repeat it in thirty different ways over as many pages of small print, and will never use an affirmative if a quadruple negative will do.

Yesterday evening Catford was introduced to Bloomsbury pastimes, a play reading having taken place in the Empire Road Salon. The piece was *Travesties*, and the cast little Moses, Judy, Paul Malet, his girlfriend and the present writer (Rackman was to have made a guest appearance, but stage fright kept him at the office till midnight). The reading did not begin till 9.30 p.m. after we had bloated ourselves into aphasia with a takeaway Indian dinner that was hot in neither sense. Having leafed through the script to find the most entertaining character, I insisted on being James Joyce, a misguided demand, for in fact the part of Henry Carr – squandered by Judy – is larger and more amusing. It was a dreary evening, for I was the only one who acted, shouting as loud as I could and ignoring the fact that Jow-enn's room was directly overhead. Paul Malet – who is hated by me and all his other philosophical contemporaries for having been appointed a lecturer in philosophy at Cambridge – was a particularly monotonous Lenin, and it was in equal measures disheartening and gratifying to find that the holder of so prestigious an academic post was unable to pronounce 'fissiparous' or to recite a simple sentence in French. When we ground to a halt at 12.15 a.m., an ill-natured discussion of the play began, Paul accusing Stoppard of pandering to the middlebrow, and Judy defending him by a characteristic jumble of half-baked *ad hominem* arguments. The result was an aporia and a tepid agreement that we must do this again.

Addendum: Leslie has moved out. I miss him terribly.

11 October

I spent last weekend with Ellénore. It was an irritating one for various reasons. First, I had a headache most of the time, induced by forced midday drinking. E has hollow legs which need constant refilling and, if you refuse to join her in ten Bloody Marys before lunch, she becomes frosty and says she refuses to drink alone. Second, she blocked the sink by washing mussels in it, and then, by implication, blamed the sea of filth on my inability to unblock the sink with a plunger. The first time I plunged, fishy water shot out of the overflow hole and hit my shirt front. I ended by washing up in the bath, like Wittgenstein. Third, the boy dragged conversation and standards of behaviour down to his infantile level. We had planned an outing on Sunday but, the weather being ominous, merely had a barbecue in E's absent mother's postage-stamp of a garden, where I kept my ears open for shrieks from Dr Hopkin's house (v.19 July). Augustus lurched manic-depressively between overweening bids for attention and, when these failed, despairing sobs. I suggested to him that he might like to eat his sausages on the seat at the other end of the garden and turn his face to the wall while doing so, which caused him to rush into the house in a tearful frenzy. As a result I had to follow and beg him, literally on my knees, to rejoin the company. This confirmed my agreement with W.C. Field's theory about people who hate kids. While Augustus was on holiday in Spain he was paid handsomely to appear in an advertisement for soap flakes. Fifty pounds of this has just been spent on a kitten, a cross between a tabby and some recondite Eastern breed. It seems a lot of money to pay for a half-caste, and I suggested to Ellénore that they had, as it were, been sold a pup. E wants to call the animal Rory, which I rejected as preposterous, so we agreed on Gridley. Gridley spent the night with us and was several times nearly crushed to death. In the mornings he and Augustus turn the Bower of Bliss into Piccadilly Circus.

Serious work has now started at NIPLES, and I am enjoying preparing answers to the problems set for discussion in tutorials. Criminal law is the most entertaining. I spent a merry morning distinguishing five concepts of intention and analysing the difference between intentions and motives. The problems ramify indefinitely and it is easy to drag in everything you know; the difficulty is to decide when to stop thinking. The decision was imposed on me several times from outside, as the Hermitage has been invaded by workmen laying a terrace. Rackman, with his infallible eye for kitsch, ordered not standard paving stones but slabs of some manmade substance with a rustic finish. Twice in the past month a lorry-load of these monstrosities has arrived, and each time Rackman sent them away because they had cracks. Finally this week a perfect set came, but the rain has been so heavy that the three workmen have spent most of the time cowering in the porch. One of them, a violent-looking Scotsman with a horrifying scar on his cheek, arrived early, so I offered him a cup of tea while he waited. 'You what?' he growled, apparently having misheard me and thinking I was getting fresh. The men's cups of tea used up all the milk, so I had to put on my Breakfast Bran some watery grey stuff for slimmers – the last trace of dear old Leslie. I took my revenge by eating the 2 lb tin of assorted biscuits that Rackman had bought to keep the men's spirits up.

Rackman recently forbade me to do my morning exercises in my bedroom on the grounds that they woke him up, so I obligingly transferred them to the dining-room. When he then claimed that they still disturbed him, I moved with a sigh into the sitting-room and started building my body on a carpet with a sub-Festival-of-Britain pattern. The other day, having found this heirloom impregnated with sweat, he told me he did not like the sitting-room being used as a gymnasium. I pointed out that for the sake of a few press-ups I was being treated like a leper and that he would have to decide whether he preferred insomnia to a bloom on the Axminster. I do not like disturbing R's sleep, for he anyway spends half the night awake with a hiatal hernia.

My dear friend Hamish rang up from Hamburg the other evening. The saying goes that, in the absence of philosophy jobs, wordy philosophers take up the law and mathsy philosophers go in for computers. The reverse is true of Hamish and me, since my Ph.D. thesis contains more mathematics than his but he is the one working for a computer firm. Mary abandoned Hamish for a bisexual architect who seems to have been an excuse rather than a reason, for she soon ditched him as well. There are many good reasons why Mary might have left Hamish, for he is only slightly less exasperating than he is endearing. In the first place, he has never regarded personal hygiene as a priority; when I used to go running with him I made sure always to stay downwind. In the second place, as already noted, he is addicted to garlic and eats whole bulbs at a go. In the third place he is indecisive to the point of mental disease. Visits to the supermarket grind to a halt as he stands like Buridan's ass, stammering inarticulately, between two indistinguishable brands of mineral water. Once, when he was staying at Frogs Cottage, the Old Dear was unwise enough to take him to the off licence. After ten minutes' hovering in front of the wines, she finally dragooned him into a choice. As they were walking away from the shop, Hamish decided that he should have bought a different wine, and insisted on going back. But, once they had changed the bottle, he decided that the first kind was better after all and, as the OD ground her teeth, they left the shop carrying the wine they had gone in with. In the fourth place he used to have drumming lessons in Finsbury Park with a Ghanaian group called Aklowa, and has ever since thundered tribal rhythms on any solid surface within reach. When he went to work in Hamburg, he bought a conga drum to play in his flat in the evenings. His neighbours were unenthusiastic, so he started beating it in a field on the outskirts of the city. However, he was soon chased away by a Bauer whose cottage was in earshot; I don't know whether he has found a more secluded place to practise. He is especially fond of playing his car. Once we drove in convoy to his house in Lewisham and, whenever we stopped at traffic lights, his Mini would sway from side to side as his arms flew about, bashing windscreen, roof and steering column. Hamish and I used to go to Goose End together to write our theses. One morning he got up later than I and, as he ate his breakfast in the dining-room (which is under my study), started hammering on the table while playing a descant with a teaspoon on his mug. I went down to remonstrate and he claimed, apparently truthfully, that he had been unaware he was doing it. We were in several ways incompatible housemates. I regularly eat a large meal at night only, while Hamish has sudden pangs of hunger, and I would find him frying the week's supply of sausages at 11.00 a.m. I also, like most people, become increasingly sleepy as the evening draws on, while Hamish becomes wider and wider awake; by midnight he would be launched into his theory of the development of the Western mind since the

Homeric age, while I looked for opportunities for sidling off to bed. The other side of his indecision is an irrational obsession with ludicrous projects. One evening in the winter, when we were almost snowed in, he suddenly decided that he had to buy Mary's brother-in-law's 1952 Humber. Goose End is in Suffolk and the car was in Herefordshire, but Hamish resolved to set off the following morning, telling me that I would have to drive him to Dunham station, from where he would embark on a journey, involving six changes, to Hereford; having picked up the old crate, he would drive it across country back to Suffolk and, when we wanted to return to London, I could drive his Mini back. He did not explain how my mother's car, which I had borrowed to get to Suffolk, would be returned to Fulham. I refused to have anything to do with the scheme, which put H in such a state that he spent the night driving round East Anglia in the snow to soothe his nerves. As a result he spent all the next afternoon asleep, which then prevented him from sleeping the following night. He attributed this insomnia, however, to the caffeine in the chocolate he had eaten before going to bed. This was one of his curious ideas about food; the house in Lewisham was full of sacks of supposedly edible seaweed, which tasted of socks, and on top of the kitchen cupboard there was a bowl of liquid with, apparently, a jellyfish floating on it; Hamish told me it was tea-beer, but did not explain what the jellyfish was doing.

Feeling too delicate to face the Lightning Omnibus, I took the train to the country this weekend, and moved up to the front carriage to be able to read in peace. I had just settled into vol. five of the Pelican *History of the Church* when a man in his fifties, looking like a member of the National Front, got in with his mouse of a wife. 'NICE AND QUIET IN HERE,' he yelled at her. 'NO JABBERERS. CAN'T STAND JABBERERS WHEN I'M TRYING TO READ. YOU MAKE SURE YOU DON'T START JABBERING' – and so on in a terrifying crescendo, till only the fear of a right hook prevented me from pointing out the self-refutation to him.

The Old Dear had kindly driven through floods to meet me at the station, and as we drove to the house she gave me the latest news of Edie. Edie, if her own words are to be believed, has an increasing number of cats in her bungalow. Yesterday she said, conjuring up an image worthy of Magritte, 'There were two little furry ones curled up in Lupin's food dishes. I don't know how they got in, for the dishes were locked. I hope they don't come back.' The old people's home cannot be far away, which saddens me, for Edie's house would presumably have to be sold to pay for her upkeep there; if she dies before the house is sold, it will go to my mother, who has promised to give it to me. But my mother told me the following encouraging story, which she heard from a girl called Mad who goes to her tap-dancing class and works in a home for geriatrics. An old lady was going to sell her house in order to go into a home. She had bought the house many years before for £750. Her daughter had it valued and told her that it was now worth £150,000. The old thing was so excited that she had a heart-attack and dropped dead on the spot. I shall be ringing the local estate agent this week.

The mention of Mad brings Simpkin's mailing list to the present writer's own rambling mind. Some years ago the list was looked after by a battleaxe called Mrs Rutter. One of the customers was a Philip Reece, M.A.,D. Phil. Mrs R was unfamiliar with academic titles, so she typed on the address label 'Philip Reece (MAD PHIL)'. He never bought anything. At one time Mrs R used to lend Max Wood her paper to read over lunch, but Max once forgot to return it and from then on they were in a state of feud. Their relation became so acrimonious that, when Mrs R was in hospital and a Get Well card was passed around the shop for everyone to sign, Max refused to do so. Mrs R never recovered, and was replaced by an obese and stupid woman called Doreen. Soon afterwards the mailing list was computerized.

18 October

Hamish has had a number of unusual jobs, having been a lumberjack, a door-to-door salesman of lavatory brushes, a postman in Stuttgart and a dyer of kippers in Aberdeen. Your high-class kipper reaches the table with its natural hue, but the boil-in-the-bag sort, if left to itself, is too grey to stimulate the taste buds and is therefore dipped in an ochreous brine at the factory. The brine is corrosive: when Hamish spilled some down his wellington boot, his foot, apart from turning yellow, was shrivelled for over a week. I told this story at a dinner in the flat of Delphine Darling, one of Ellénore's circle of Kensington divorcees. Most of these ladies have names as precious as Delphine's (another is called Jacintha, or Jack for short) and take revenge on their children, Augustus having playmates called Peregrine, Tatton and Ebenezer. DD is a professional cook – though this was hard to infer from her rice – and gave me a marblized visiting card saying 'Delphine Darlings (no apostrophe) Dainty Delicacies' in letters small enough to exclude the possibility of presbyopic clients. The flat being in Cranley Gardens, I also told the story of Lord and Lady Power, whose young son sleepwalked off a Cranley Gardens balcony and plunged to his death. This led somehow or other to my retailing an anecdote I heard from Dr Conrad Hone about a musician who could only achieve an orgasm by watching young men sit up in a coffin. As a result I was pronounced 'hysterical' by DD – not, I hope, in Freud's and Breuer's sense.

The dinner was one of a giddy round of engagements Ellénore had prepared for me this week; by Saturday I felt like the Queen returning from a state visit. Rackman's interpretation was that she (Ellénore, not Her Majesty) was 'showing me off'. The night before, we went to dinner in another part of the Royal Borough, at the house of the Hon. Arabella Bassett, a placid, amiable and elephantine lady who has replaced her husband with a carpenter called Dick. At the end of the evening Dick launched into a lager-wally harangue about the virtues of privatization while Arabella chuckled indulgently. He is self-consciously bluff: recently Ellénore had him round to her flat to look at the hall, which needs decorating. 'How can I stop the children ruining the new paint?' she asked. 'Send them to a concentration camp' was Dick's suggestion. Cyril Beamish, an antiquarian bookseller, was also at the dinner and strained my faltering sense of loyalty with questions about the Simpkin power-structure. The other two guests were an entrepreneur wearing rings, who looked as if he had started his career selling lead behind the White City stadium, and his wife Zoë – a former model with a mirthless rictus, her face a death's-head impastoed with cosmetics. Unfortunately Zoë sat next to me and damaged my inner right ear by unpredictably screaming at intervals with demonic laughter. Although in her forties, she has just taken an O-level in maths, which she scraped through, and Ellénore became angry when I referred to her as the Gauss of Gloucester Road. The food was creditable, given that Arabella had broken her wrist the day before, and was marred only by the flatus of a newly retired guidedog she has adopted. I wondered whether guidedogs were trained to fart so that their owners could find them easily.

On Friday evening I was introduced to Ellénore's mother, a grand old French émigrée from the Côte de Guermantes, who lives in a poky bijou flat full of fine pieces. Her voice is both soft and imperious, and she clearly expects all other conversation to stop when she makes an observation about the weather – as she frequently does. The old girl had gone to munificent lengths for a family supper, serving salmon mousse, casserole of pigeon, and ice cream with chocolate sauce. Augustus, present in his pyjamas, was at his most fractious, exclaiming that he couldn't stand the sight of the mousse and comparing the casserole to diarrhoea. Fortunately he fell so sound asleep on his doting grandmother's knee that he was put to bed in her four-poster, so E and I were free to molest each other till the onset of the string of gossiping phone calls that seem to be a regular feature of her Saturday mornings. One of these was from her friend Campaspe Walters, who narrated how a girl-friend had rung the doorbell, having come to ask for a bowl of sugar or something. Campaspe's husband Edward was alone in the house and came to the door in his dressing gown. As he looked through the peep-hole at eye level, the girlfriend peered through the letterbox at genital level and, Edward's dressing gown not being properly tied up, received a shock. Ellénore insists on letting Gridley into the bedroom, and on Friday night he sat at the foot of the bed learning skills which the vet is shortly to prevent him from ever practising. He has an irritating habit of teetering along the bedhead and then falling off, landing on one's face; he also woke me up more than once by licking my hair and nipples. Another new resident in the flat is a dopy lodger called Lucy (pronounced Leecy) whose rent consists partly of babysitting. She is a student at the Prue Leith School of Cookery and regularly produces unflushable turds; I do not know whether these facts are related. Augustus and I have both rushed from the lavatory and protested loudly to Ellénore, who suggested that I have a word with L. But, as L makes Fatima Whitbread look like a stick-insect, I have decided merely to avert eyes and nostrils. Poor Lucy suffers from terminal listlessness. As she is a cookery student, Ellénore sometimes asks her if she would like the recipe for such-and-such a dish. 'No thanks,' L replies, or 'not much'. She was cowed shortly after her arrival by having heard E's ma refer to her, during an *ultra vires* inspection of her room, as a slut.

It would have been wiser to shun Ellénore this week, as she has been struggling against a viral infection that has caused her glands to swell, her temperature to rise and her doctor to give her pills that make her vomit, but I tried to disguise my terror of infection as solicitude.

117

There is, as they say, a lot of it about, NIPLES being full of invalids. Tutorials have now started, and we gather in groups of ten to advise, e.g., an imaginary aged house-keeper called Gladys on whether she can sue for an annuity under a trust. My subtle distinctions seem to be wasted both on my classmates and on the teachers, one of whom (Mr Taylor) does not know the difference between inferring and implying, and another (Mrs Erasmus) said that you can't prove a negative; I pointed out that I could just as easily prove that she was *not* wearing a hat as that she *was*. Friday's tutorial on tort was cancelled on the outrageous ground of bad weather, but the cancellation was a relief, tort being the most dispiriting branch of the law. After an hour of Ortonesque cases in which blind men fall down inadequately fenced manholes, surgeons crush babies' heads with forceps, fishwives suffer miscarriages from the sight of motorcyclists' remains scattered over the road, and physically handicapped persons suffer severe injuries through the practical jokes of puerile fellow-employees, the student is reaching for his paper bag. Tort lectures are the law student's equivalent of the medical student's anatomy practicals.

Mary came to dinner on Tuesday, having returned from a tour of the Pacific with the orchestra. (It seems that the major orchestras live out of suitcases, a thrill that must pale after a few years.). M has a good eye for the bizarre, but her memory is so feeble that Rackman and I heard few anecdotes that we had not already read on her postcards. She sent us a jolly one from New Zealand with a picture of some mud pools and a printed caption saying, 'Thermal mud expresses itself in weird shapes.' On this card she told us how she went to a concert given by Maoris in the local meeting house. The room was dark and, for some reason she did not explain, full of steam. Through the mists she could see an eerie shape which she took to be the statue of a god or a skull left from a cannibal feast, but on closer inspection it turned

118

out to be a bust of Queen Victoria mounted on a Maori pedestal. On Tuesday she told us that there is an epidemic of VD among koalas.

Rackman and I must have given Mary a good press, for Jow-enn had been anxious to meet her, saying that she sounded 'so sensible and mature'. J was therefore present at table, despite Rackman's having taken against her and threatening (to me) to evict her at the end of the month. Things came to a head when he presented her with an electricity bill which she thought exorbitant. It is not feasible for a lodger to prove fraud against Rackman, for his bills are so complicated that it would be beyond one's arithmetical ability to establish the claim. Jow-enn preferred to ring up her psychotherapist (a lapsed Catholic priest) and weep down the line about R's avarice and cruelty. It would have been a wiser financial decision to pay up at once, for she was on the phone for over thirty minutes, Rackman charges calls by the second and the good father consults at £15 per hour (but perhaps therapy by phone is free). In the event, she flung the money for the electricity at R and flounced off to bed. I shall not be sorry to see her go, for her obsessive rituals of washing are getting on my nerves. The other night, having heard her emerge from the bathroom for the fifth time, I went to brush my teeth, but she sneaked in again for another manic ablution before I could get there. The wash basin is by the door, so I tiptoed up and bellowed through the keyhole, an inch from her right ear, 'WILL YOU PASS OUT MY TOOTHBRUSH.' I am hoping, since she shrieked and came out shaking, that this has cured her of her obsession.

24 October

East Anglia being under water, the Old Dear and I were confined to London for the weekend, so on Sunday I had her round to tea. She was displeased that there was no cake, for the last time she came Rackman, in a rare flash of good humour, had baked a Victoria sponge in her honour. As it was, she had to make do with the remains of the packet of chocolate Hobnobs that Jow-enn had bought for me in an effort to cement an alliance against our landlord. Rackman is becoming impossibly gloomy. When I complained that the water was lukewarm, he replied 'Fuck off', and when it turned out that Julius, who is coming to stay, will be arriving off the boat-train tonight, while I am in the country, Rackman showed clear signs of being unprepared to receive him in my absence. As a result J will be met at Victoria by a Tannoy announcement that he is to spend his first night in London on the street. R's spleen may be explained by the fact that he has been giving dinner to several women recently; he is a closet misogynist. He spent most of Sunday digging a mysterious trench in the garden. This cheered him up a bit, and in the evening he drove Mary and me to an Indian restaurant in Herne Hill. Bloated with biryani, I spent the hours before bed reading *Der goldne Topf*, which Transistor gave me. I learned German in order to read German books, and now read German books to keep up my German. Exercise for the reader: is this a vicious or a virtuous circle?

On Tuesday Mary took me to a concert given by a Hungarian pianist whose name seemed to be Coccyx. He played with Magyar gusto, looked like a little boy and should change his barber. The recital was at the Law Society; perhaps M invited me because she thought I would feel at home. If I wanted to be a member of a club for old buffers, the LS would not be a bad bet, for it would cost only sixty-odd pounds a year; *World Affairs Magazine* pays about £400 to allow Abram to play snooker once a year at the Reform. The LS also has some interesting majolica cornices. I was dismayed, however, by the other members of the audience; most of the men looked like Dr Cameron, had wives with blue hair and rustled their programmes. I hope they were on an outing for provincial solicitors, for, if I am going to be surrounded by such types at Savage Borman, I shall resign now. (At dinner the other day a solicitor from Slaughter and May told me that Savage B was notable for being a firm 'wholly without style'. I was uncertain what this meant; perhaps everyone at Slaughters sports a monocle and spats.) I don't like to think what these old boys would say if they heard how the National Institute of Professional Legal Studies was spending the funds of its social club. Each year a certain sum is allotted for students to start societies, and this time the only application has been for money to start a Lesbian Society. I am seeking financial support for a 'Young Solicitors Against Lesbianism' club.

I have just received a second set of offprints of 'Substitutional Quantification and Modal Operators', a paper of mine that has been published in *Quaere* – a journal of breathtaking obscurity, printed in characters apparently designed for the visually handicapped. That I have been given a second set is due to my having written to the editor, Professor Louis Kuntz, to complain that in the first set, and – *ohimè* – in the copies of the journal, half the logical symbols had been garbled and the other half omitted. A reader with (i) an advanced degree in mathematical logic, (ii) a sabbatical year, (iii) the conviction that the paper marked a turning-point in Western thought and (iv) the detective powers of Sherlock Holmes might have worked out what the paper was saying. To anyone else, the publishers have made it incomprehensible. Kuntz's explanation why some of the symbols had been left out was that the printer's font did not contain them, the printer had therefore pasted them in on bits of paper, and the bits of paper had fallen off. The paper was originally read at a conference on '*les fondements de la mathématique*' at the Université de Lille III. This prestigious international event is held biennially, alternately at Lille and at the Middlesex

Polytechnic. The Université de Lille III stands beside a motorway on the outskirts of the city and was obviously erected out of breeze blocks one weekend in the early sixties. In an attempt at humanization, the surfaces of the buildings have been covered with rusticated prefab panels of stone-ite (similar to Rackman's terrace) and, to inject some *Gemeinschaft*, a housing estate was put up next to the university, so that now the bustlings of the academics are watched aimlessly by unemployed Algerians leaning out of twentieth-storey windows. When I arrived, on a Sunday evening, the place was deserted. The Algerians were watching telly, the academics were miles away and a few paper cups blew about the empty piazza. Having waited in vain at an unmanned desk marked '*Accueil*' (which Hamish, another *conférencier*, pronounced 'Akweel' ('*tilleul*' he pronounces 'teel-weel'), I wandered off and eventually found a concierge wearing a Walkman. I bellowed that I was looking for the halls of residence, and he sent me off on Lille's new metro – which advertised itself as the city's pride – to an identical wasteland in a suburb at the other end of town. As usual in French universities, the rooms were too small for a hamster and you had to take your own roll of paper with you into the lavatory. To remind the denizens that they were in a bastion of culture, the corridors were named after luminaries of French literature. I was pleased to be on Montaigne, though Hamish found himself on Engels (shome mishtake shurely). As philosophy conferences go (not far), it was an enjoyable event, and I befriended a well-known philosopher of science by telling him the story of Conrad Hone's visit to the first birthday party of a fellow-philosopher's son. Hone, childless Director of Studies in Philosophy at an Oxford college, went to the toy shop and donnishly asked, 'Have you something suitable for someone with a mental age of one?' The assistant's face fell in sympathy. 'Oh dear,' she said, 'how old is he really?' 'One,' Hone replied. By the end of the conference the seminars had fallen behind schedule, and I was forced to give my forty-five-minute paper in five, while an eminent Belgian philosopher, who had driven in specially from Louvain, was told that there was no time for his talk at all. White with rage, he got straight into his car again.

1 November

Ellénore came to Frogs Cottage last weekend, where we spent most of the time spooning. She kindly cooked a large dinner, which she insisted on eating by candle-light. I managed to dig out some filthy candles that the Old Dear keeps for powercuts, and there was nearly a domestic tragedy when the cat climbed on the table, waved its tail through the flames and filled the room with the stench of burning fur; but the little dear seemed undisturbed by its bald patch. After dinner E and I lay by the fire and undressed as far as the Siberian tem-perature would allow. 'Have you done this with anyone else?' she asked. 'No,' I lied, turning my mind's eye away from Rebecca's naked form lying on the same stretch of carpet, and from Annie's to the left behind the chair. Dry martinis prevented me from fully exploiting the situation, and in fact my libido, faltering at best, is at its lowest ebb in the evening. My lack of vigour is an obstacle to our relationship; nights chez Ellénore leave me shattered, for she and her sons need less sleep than Mrs Thatcher. On Wednesday, after a night of torturing brevity, I was so tired that I suffered auditory halluci-nations while reading Megarry and Wade's *Law of Real Property* in the Institute's library.

In our brief moments out of bed during the weekend, we went for a walk and I tested E's loyalty by taking her shopping in Knatworth. The walk was short, for E has very short legs. Being so stunted, she could not see what was the other side of the grass bank at the back of the house; I told her that there was a great inland sea, and she smiled tiredly. In Knatworth she bought some little cakes for Edie (she was much impressed by my ability to keep a straight face as Edie burbled senile gibberish), and managed to drag all the shop girls into a merry conversation about the suitability of the different kinds of coconut kisses for octogenarian dentition. This made me uneasy, for I like to shop and walk through the streets with the aloofness of Dr Kien. My supercilious manner tends to keep people at a distance, but sometimes it misfires. Usually the last seat to be taken in a crowded tube carriage is the one next to mine. Recently, however, I was travelling on the Northern Line to Golders Green and was alone in the carriage, with my briefcase on the next seat. A man got in at Belsize Park and walked up to the seat with the case on it. He stared at the case, then at me, and then said 'Excuse me' in a threatening voice. I feebly moved the case and spent the rest of the journey staring at the advertisements while he sat next to me. The case, which cost a great deal of money, tends to excite envy and may have been responsible for another nasty incident involving trains that happened as I returned to the Empire Road Athenaeum on Sunday night. As I was running to catch the 18.45 Orpington service, the brass clasps of the case's handle twinkling in the last rays of an autumn sunset, a youth yelled 'Yuppie wanker' and various other things. After I had leapt on to the train, it sat in the station for some time, and the youth had time to catch up with me. 'Oy, wanker!' he shouted, knocking on the window. I smiled nervously and waved, then pretended to read the *London Review of Books* as the other passengers sniggered. Example three: at Liverpool Street, while I was looking at the overhead train indicator, I knocked into a rough man and pretended not to have noticed. 'Up your fuckin' arse!' he spat. 'Up yours,' I replied, walking away. 'What!' he exploded, and started pursuing me. I walked more and more quickly round the station, and finally shook him off by darting into the gents.

*

124

Julius, the reader will remember, has no faults. He therefore showed no ill will towards me for having left him unsheltered on his arrival in London. We met on Tuesday at Abram's office, and A's assistant recoiled as Julius – who measures six foot six in all directions – loomed up at the door. The assistant has just completed his degree in natural science at Cambridge and is useful to Abram, who is Science Editor despite having not even an O-level in any scientific subject. A, J, and I went to dinner at Chez Gerard, which is only distinguished from a Berni Inn by the facts (a) that the staff try to make the diners speak French, (b) that it is ten times as expensive and (c) that the leathery steak is garnished with garlic instead of a tomato. As a result of (c) Ellénore, whom I went on to visit, made a fuss about my breath – but she is namby-pamby about odours in general. At the weekend she complained, preposterously, that my bedroom smelled musty.

It is a sign of a lodger always to cook the same simple meal. Since moving into the Athenaeum I have cooked pasta so often that the sight of it now puts me in a rage, and I long to dine out for a change of food. When therefore Louise, who gave me dinner on Wednesday, announced that she was serving spinach and ricotta ravioli, I was silently indignant, and I could barely contain myself when the Old Dear produced spaghetti Bolognese on Friday. Louise lives in a minute flat in Kilburn; the architect responsible for converting the original small house into three rabbit hutches must have had difficulty fitting the rudimentary domestic conveniences into the ten square feet available for each hutch, for L's bathroom sticks out into her sitting-room, a partition of quarter-inch plywood separating the feet of any bather from the company round the fireside. When you first visit, you wonder where the kitchen is, and then notice a stove and sink behind the sitting-room bookshelf. Moses and Judy were there, and Moses was complaining about his neighbour in Aneurin Bevan

House. She is an unmarried mother, unemployed, with low intelligence and a yapping dog, and keeps knocking on M's door to ask for a few quid. This, M said, was bad enough, but the worst is that at night she leans out of her kitchen window with a fag, the smoke blowing into the little fellow's bedroom.

On Thursday evening I gave a dinner in Julius's honour, inviting him, Abram, Samantha, Ellénore and the Old Dear, who is a great admirer of Julius and is convinced that he is going to be a US senator. When he was living in London a few years ago, he had the OD's cats – then kittens – to stay for a week while she was abroad. 'Just think, little dears,' she said as she took them home, 'you'll be able to say you stayed with a senator.' Julius has never had any intention of going into politics. The dinner was, as always, an appalling effort, despite Ellénore's bringing the soup and the OD's bringing a trifle. The two came in E's car, thus enabling them to get acquainted in my absence, which may or may not be a good thing. E also gave the OD a lift home and, as she was manoeuvring out of the parking space, her car rolled backwards with a crunch into Rackman's. I have not dared to look at R's motor since. He was not present, having to attend a business dinner; it is to be hoped that this indicates an imminent partnership, for the resulting increase in income would give his lodgers a watertight argument for a reduction in rent. I nobly asked Jow-enn to the dinner and was rewarded by her telling me that she was already going to a concert. She returned in time for the pudding, however, and was closely scrutinized by the other guests, who had heard so much about her. Despite being a musician, she did not join in the chorus of Happy Birthday; it turned out to be Julius's twenty-eighth, and Abram had brought a cake with 'Julius' written on it. J, although he has lungs like barrage balloons, took three puffs to blow out the candles. (Edie needed only two to extinguish her eightieth birthday cake.) Samantha, who is charming, looks like a semi-detached housewife from Ruislip, but it turns out that this is a disguise, for Abram, when he was taken to her parents' house in Norfolk for the weekend, found that the car had drawn up in front of a stately home the size of Blenheim Palace. As S led Abram along the echoing corridors, she identified the portraits of a string of noble ancestors, most of whom had been beheaded. Life at Château Salisbury-Loake is formal, and Abram had to wear black tie for dinner. When the ladies left the table, he rose to follow them and had to be dragged back for his port. The formality extends to sexual mores, Abram and Samantha being put in separate wings. Samantha's brother and his girlfriend were given the same treatment, but the brother, overcome by desire in the middle of the night, set off on tiptoe in his pyjamas for a passionate encounter. While doing so, he triggered the burglar alarm, and a fleet of police cars roared into the front quadrangle with blue lights flashing at two in the morning. What the Salisbury-Loakes made of Abram, a north London Jewish boy with Middle European refugee parents, is unrecorded, but A clearly relished his weekend with the toffs, the more so as he has a theory – the details of which escape me – that he himself is 454th in line to the English throne. It is alarming to contemplate the chain of 454 accidents that would result in King Abram I being crowned at Westminster Abbey.

8 November

Conrad Hone, when he was under the weather, wanted some Combination H, a herbal remedy for flu. Misremembering the name, he asked me to buy him some Preparation H, which is a medicine for piles. When I asked for it in the health shop, the assistant said, 'Do you want the ointment or the suppositories?' The other customers smirked. 'I don't know,' I replied flushing, 'it's for a friend.' The assistant had obviously heard this

127

before and, to put me out of my misery, proposed the ointment. When I gave it to Dr Hone, he rubbed some on the end of his nose. The assistant at the shop was a bad advertisement for health foods, as he suffered from advanced Parkinson's disease; he got me the ointment by pointing himself towards the shelf and shaking his way towards it. Healthfood shops and restaurants are frequently staffed by unhealthy specimens whose vigour and complexion would benefit from a plate of red meat. I have accompanied little Moses to a macrobiotic bakery where we spent half an hour of apoplexy while a listless girl with a sickly smile of yellow teeth wondered how to open the till. I met with the same service on Monday evening, when I ate a slice of quiche made of cement at a wholefood restaurant in Covent Garden before going to *Figaro* with Ellénore. It is widely held that *Il Trovatore* is the hardest opera to follow, but in my view it is a piece of cake compared with *Le Nozze*.

After the opera I stayed the night with Ellénore, thereby continuing my neglect of Julius, who was now staying at the Empire Road Hospice for the Depressed. I hate having people to stay and am therefore a casual host. When Julius came to Goose End for the weekend, I worked most of the time and made the Old Dear drive him to the station. And, when on Wednesday he set off from Empire Road for the airport, the nearest I came to helping him carry his cases to the station was to say, as I stood on the doorstep in my dressing gown, 'I suppose I should have offered to help you carry your cases to the station.' He would have done better to stay with the Salvation Army. On the day after the party I gave in his honour, I did not get up till noon, and found him huddled over the dining-room gas fire in his overcoat, the central heating having gone off hours before. He had been unable to have a bath, as Rackman had set the thermostat for the water only slightly above freezing point. The tiny truckle bed we assigned to Julius, in the garret that used to be occupied by dear old Leslie, had no blankets, and the sleeping bag I had stolen from Rackman's cupboard was too small for him to get into; being as tall as a negro basketball champion and as wide as Cyril Smith, he overhung the bed in all directions. He nevertheless donated a bottle of malt whisky in gratitude for our hospitality; I waited until I had the bottle in my hands before telling him that the other two occupants were teetotal. Rackman certainly did not deserve a present, having (a) made a fuss about my lending Julius a key and (b) complained that J woke him up by walking about overhead (J pointed out to me that *he* had been kept awake by R's snoring).

On Thursday Rackman announced that he is increasing the rent by thirty per cent, and was unmoved when I reminded him (i) that this is roughly 700 per cent the rate of inflation, (ii) I am on a fixed income of £0 pa and (iii) he has had a substantial raise this year. Since he has repeatedly said that I am a model tenant, it is unlikely that he is trying to make me leave, but that may well be the result of his greed. He obviously feels guilty about the increase, as his voice quavered when he announced it. R and I were to dine with Mary this week, but he cried off and Mary proposed instead that she and I go to the Kabuki theatre. 'Will she take Noh for an answer?' Rackman asked, trying to make me laugh off his extortion, but I did not have the opportunity to find out, as she too cancelled. In consequence I have had a week of quiet evenings, which is as well, for I have a pile of tutorial problems to prepare answers to. For example: 'Don, a man of low intelligence, sees Vic carry a television set out of a house and place it in the boot of a car. [In these questions the defendant always has a name beginning with D, and the victim one beginning with V.] Thinking that Vic is a thief, he tells him to stop. Vic replies, "Get lost, Dumbo, before I give you a belting." Don thereupon flies into a rage and hits Vic with a wheel brace which is lying nearby. Vic's skull is fractured and an ambulance is called to take him to hospital. On the way, however, the ambulance crashes and Vic is killed. There is evidence to the effect that, but for his fractured skull, Vic would probably have survived the accident. Consider Don's liability for Vic's death.' Mr Judd, who set this question, is also witty in lectures, though he does not like to be upstaged: he was brusque when, during a discussion of a crime involving a chapatti pan, a student interrupted to point out that there are two ts in 'chapatti'. Being reserved, I am only slowly getting acquainted with my fellow pupils. I have warmed to the token black, who greeted me with 'Hi, prof!' as I glared at her over my spectacles.

On Saturday I bumped into Will Fish, a boon companion at Oxford, who directed many plays while he was a student and has ever since been sweeping the stage at various fringe theatres. His bohemian life is epitomized by a holiday he spent in Italy. In one *pensione* he was discovered at three in the morning, buggering the landlord's seventeen-year-old son. The landlord kicked him out, throwing his clothes out of the window after him. In another, he got up in the night for a pee and, being unable to find the light switch, stepped into the bidet. His big toe got stuck in the plug hole and he fell forward on to the wash basin which, under his weight, came away from the wall, causing a fountain of water to gush into the room. Whether or not as a result of having to pay damages for this accident, he soon after ran out of money and went without food for several days. This provoked the first hallucination of his life, a luminous baguette filled with mortadella and salad, hovering before his eyes as he lay in bed. Will's domestic life was not easy. He, his father and mother and two sisters all lived in Hendon in a tiny cottage, a remnant of pre-Northern Line days. All the family were large and father and mother spent much of the time fighting furiously, getting through a complete set of crockery a week. When Fish *père* became a threat to life, Will would lock him out of the house; he was senior partner of a large accountancy firm. Mrs Fish was a kind and motherly

130

lady and has since died of cancer. She was a bastion of the tiny Hendon branch of the Liberal Party and, a few hours after she had died, a couple of Liberals, unaware that she was even ill, called at the house. 'Is Mrs Fish in?' they asked. 'In a manner of speaking,' Will replied, for his mother's corpse was lying in the room upstairs. 'Can we speak to her then, please?' 'No, I'm afraid she has just died.' The Liberals were unable to take this in. 'We only want a quick word,' they persisted. 'Look, you can't speak to her. She's *dead*.' There was an embarrassed pause. 'Well, can we leave a poster, then?' one of them asked nervously. Will shut the door in their face. As he turned to rejoin his grief-sticken family, a leaflet with the beaming face of the local Liberal candidate slid gingerly through the letter-box. Will has since married and has two teenage stepchildren. Before we parted on Saturday, he asked me to tell my mother that he had not burnt Sausage's whiskers. I had no idea what he was talking about until he reminded me that, during a party twelve years ago, the Old Dear had found him cuddling Sausage with a cigarette lighter (unlit) in his hand; the OD then noticed that the whiskers on one side of S's face were shrivelled. Having always been suspicious of Will, she accused him of having singed the whiskers with his lighter. In fact Sausage had singed them himself by leaning against a hot pipe behind the boiler. I passed on Will's message to the OD, assuming that after all this time she would be as nonplussed by it as I had been, but she immediately snapped, 'Of course Will burned them!'

14 November

One of the plays Will directed at Oxford was *Hamlet*. The cast was small, each actor playing several roles. I was Rosencrantz and Guildenstern – or, more strictly, spoke the lines of both. The part of my companion was reduced to a silent one, which we thought of assigning to a dog, but it was played in the event by a stage hand. I was also Fortinbras, and was complimented by members of the audience on the breadth of my shoulders for such a young man, no-one realizing that my cuirass – an RSC cast off – was two feet wider than my own willowy torso. We took the production on a tour of northern French universities, which were at least as depressing as the Université de Lille III (v. 24 October) and still bore their spray-painted slogans from the late sixties. When we set off we were grossly under-rehearsed, and in the first university – Rheims – we managed to get into a loop in Act I, playing the second Ghost scene three times. The audience seemed not to notice, but the performance was being filmed and the additional running time was presumably detected on replay. At Rouen we were reviewed in the local paper, which said, 'If this is the best Oxford can do, we never want to see them again.' Among the personnel were a rough man called Brian Cox (the only student at Oxford whose father was a boiler maker from Warrington), Susie Griffiths (notable for her laugh: tss tss), Rackman (who played Polonius – having developed middle-age spread at the age of sixteen, he was always in demand to play old buffers), Jack Korn (the stage-manager, whose favourite expressions – as is the way with stage crews – were 'Naff' and 'Can't be done') and Rita Paleomylites, of whom more below. We travelled around in a Mini van, and I now have only random memories of the tour: (1) When we were nearing Dover on the outward journey, Rackman produced a tupperware box of egg and olive sandwiches. The van was hot and the sandwiches had been put in the box the night before. When he took off the lid, the van filled with a mephitic gas; we screeched to a halt and all piled out until it had dispersed. Rackman then ate the sandwiches. (2) We stopped for a pee in a lay-by and Rackman tried to balance like a sealion on an oil drum that was lying on its side. He fell over backwards and involuntarily performed a perfect somersault. (3) On the autoroute to

Rouen Rita shaved Rackman's legs in the back of the van. (4) In Amiens (which Will insisted on pronouncing Amion) I received a message that my father was dying of a brain tumour. (5) We stopped at a country church. I slipped into the confessional and gave confession to Rita, who was drunk. (6) On the way back we made a detour to Margate. Sitting on the sands on a drizzly March afternoon, I tried to fool Rita into eating a sandwich with a dead starfish in it.

Rita was Oxford's *femme fatale*: everyone desired her, and most were granted their desire. (Once, at the end of a punting party, everyone had got out of the punt except Rita, who said, 'There's still an oar in the boat.' 'There certainly is,' Will murmured.) Rita and I had an affair for a month or two at Oxford, my main attraction in her eyes being that I had a room; she was for some reason accommodationless at the time. She found the room less desirable after she fell asleep wearing my towelling dressing gown in front of the gas fire and went up in flames. In return for information about my sexual preferences she revealed that she liked to be tied up, so one weekend at Frogs Cottage I rummaged around the garden shed looking for lengths of rope and hoping that the Old Dear would not appear and ask me what I was doing. I discovered that there is little pleasure for the untied party when his partner is trussed like a Christmas turkey. Rita abandoned me when I was in bed with tonsilitis. In fact, in the two weeks I lay there, I was more or less ignored by everybody. Abram visited once with a half grapefruit which he said he owed me. My only other visitors were a drip called Cundy, who was to have my room the following term, and his girlfriend. They only came to inspect the premises, and went out leaving the windows open (it was a cold day and my temperature was high) and the taps running. My only distractions were a box-set of Sibelius symphonies – I have been depressed by Sibelius ever since – and the steam radio by the bed. Every so often a valve in the radio would explode and smoke would drift across my face, but it never interfered with the reception. Rita has since become a reasonably successful actress; the Old Dear and I recently saw her on the box in a play. 'Isn't that Rita?' said the OD as R started to reveal her bosoms on the screen. 'I'll be able to tell you when she has unbuttoned her blouse,' I replied, but the OD did not find that amusing. She hated Rita, the rot having set in when the OD found me washing dishes and Rita not drying but lounging in the kitchen chair, smoking a cigarette through a long holder.

At Oxford I did much more acting than philosophy, as I was suffering from a delayed adolescent anxiety about work. One year I went with a group to the Edinburgh Fringe, where we performed many lousy modern plays including Gertrude Stein's *Doctor Faustus Lights the Lights*. The audience for this consisted of two graduate students, who sat with the text on their knee. I was the Doctor, and did not give of my best, having made myself sick on three Arbroath smokies shortly before. Eighteen of us stayed in a flat whose owner had fraudulently been led to believe that he was letting it to an academic couple attending the Festival. All but the lucky few slept on the floor and were woken in the mornings by a splash of urine in the face from Susie's enuretic puppy. I discovered a pipe which stuck out under the sink and which, on being blown down, caused the plumbing throughout the large Georgian building to resound like the organ in the Albert Hall. Following complaints about this from neighbours, the owner paid a surprise visit and, having discovered eighteen toothbrushes in the bathroom mug, evicted us.

The screen now goes misty and we move forward ten years. This week I was forced to recognize how viciously competitive I am. At the Institute we were given marks for our first piece of written work; I received eight out of twenty and subsided into an agony of humiliation and self-doubt. The essay concerned the doctrine of promissory estoppel, which neither is clearly stated in the textbook nor has been adequately explained by Mr Lees, the lecturer. When I asked him to enunciate the doctrine, he started 'Promissory estoppel is when . . .' and went on to give an example. Someone displaying so shaky a grasp of the difference between an instance and a definition would do well to read a Platonic dialogue or two. Undaunted by this conspiracy of impressionism, in my essay I ventured North's formulation of the doctrine – an admirable display of subtlety involving a fourfold conditional clause. 'NO', wrote Lees in the margin. Doubtless I would have scored more points by following the tradition of vagueness. Lees also took it upon himself to 'correct' some properly spelled words. A fourth doctor of philosophy has come out in my tutorial group – a reticent and attractive woman called Teresa, who wrote a thesis about cancer. We doctors hence constitute forty per cent of the class. Interestingly, it emerged from Lees's assessment that we also form the bottom of the class.

Although I am not speaking to Rackman, on account of the increase in rent, I accompanied him to Mary's for dinner on Monday. The food was less elaborate than she had intended, for she had had a car crash and was forced to shop on a bicycle. Mary is always having motor accidents and they are always the other person's fault; I don't know what an actuary would make of this. Both M and R being teetotal, there was not a drop of liquor in the house, and I had to go to the off licence for a can of beer. Transistor, when she returned to Germany, bequeathed to Mary her hamster, and we devoted our attention to it when the conversation ran out. Transistor had cruelly kept the animal in a drawer covered with chicken-wire (Rackman, referring to the war, said he would have expected no better from a German) and it must have suffered anomie when placed in the futuristic cage that

135

Mary bought for it in Peckham. There are three storeys, a little house stuffed with wadding, a series of ladders and a wheel. The hamster, however, is too fat to enjoy the facilities. Rackman, recognizing a fellow weight-ignorer, kept feeding it pieces of Fruit and Nut. The hamster was too polite to refuse, and stored the chocolate in its cheeks, regurgitating it after we left.

While we were there, Hamish rang up and sounded wan; he is clearly trying to disguise from himself the fact that he hates Hamburg, computers, computer engineers and living alone. He is always making Mary send him things which he claims he can't buy in Germany and which are stored in his secret cupboard in the house they still jointly own. The latest relief parcel contained (1) a stroboscope, (2) a bottle of Essence of Wild Oats, (3) assorted vitamin pills and (4) a book on how to achieve a mucus-free diet. I thought it tactless to ask Mary about the wild oats, but queried the other items. As regards the stroboscope, she explained that Hamish did not want it for scientific purposes: he just liked looking at it. Rackman and I both warned of the danger of epileptic fits. Surely vitamins are obtainable in Germany? I asked. Yes, she replied, but Hamish thinks they are not as healthy as British vitamins. She pointed out that she has to send the pills wrapped in a way that prevents them from rattling, for the Germans, to protect their pharmaceutical industry, forbid the importation of drugs and kindred substances. As for the mucus-free diet, she was not sure whether this was a diet that contained no mucus or one that would cause mucus to dry up in the eater.

Yesterday morning I went to my dentist, Mr Prynne. He is a creep, and I continue my patronage only because I am too lazy to find a replacement. The Old Dear has recommended a Chinese called Mr K. Lim (misreading his name, she addressed him on her visit as Mr Klim), but I have rejected him on the grounds (a) that his surgery is in Tooting and (b) that he is not on the National Health. However, Prynne's attachment to the NHS seems purely nominal: he will look into your gob for the statutory minimum price, but charges £1 a second from the moment he sticks anything in it. To soothe his clients he keeps tortoises in the garden and plays Radio 2 in the surgery, and, in a misconceived attempt at bonhomie, he will address you by some nickname. My mother jilted him for Lim because she was fed up with being called Young Lady, and he regularly enrages an elderly male patient we know by calling him Squire. I used to be called Sonny, but yesterday was promoted to Doctor and treated to a physiological commentary on the state of my gums. I pointed out that I was a doctor not of medicine but of philosophy, whereupon Prynne belaboured me with questions about philosophy, as his son is about to read it at university. I was unable to answer, for he had put a sucking machine in my mouth. Garrulous dentists are even more tiresome than garrulous barbers. I had become literally long in the tooth, so Prynne filled in the carious gap between enamel and gum, using an instrument looking like a miniature hair dryer which lit up in purple and emitted beeping noises. He communicated with his nurse by whistles, like a shepherd at a sheep dog trial. Not surprisingly, she often failed to interpret him correctly and, when she handed him the wrong spike, he would throw it on the floor in irritation. Dentistry is supposed to be the profession with the highest rate of suicides, but, if Prynne were found on the surgery floor with his head drilled through, I should suspect the nurse of justifiable homicide.

3 November

On Sunday evening I met one of Ellénore's cousins, a portrait painter called Oliver, whose quick brain and sense of humour are partly concealed by a shabby suit and bumbling manner. He spoke in a gurgling voice from the back of the throat and oscillated between aphorism and stuttering inarticulacy. The inarticulacy was excusable, as he had just crossed the Channel in heavy seas; I admired his ability to put away a plate of pasta and three large gins so soon afterwards. A photograph of a wave is enough to make me seasick. When I was on a cross-Channel ferry with Abram and Rackman, they persuaded me to have a sit-down lunch with them. We were at a table for four. The fourth diner, a stranger, was a man with a severe facial tic that jerked his mouth away from his soup spoon whenever he raised it. Abram and Rackman were shaking with silent merriment, but my eyes were fixed in dread on a gauge that measured the degree the ship was tilting. Soon the sea was so rough that the gauge could not register the incline. A passenger at the next table was tipped over backwards and knocked unconscious. Unable to stare any longer at my gammon and pineapple (Rackman had already pressed half a pound of cherries on me before lunch), I went up on deck and was soon convalescing in the breeze. A man, leaning on the rail next to me, turned and smiled and suddenly – waaagh – vomited a stomach-full which the wind whisked past my face. Cherries have been involved in several of my experiences of seasickness. When, at age eighteen, I was touring the Cyclades, I was befriended by a German and his two daughters, who invited me on to their yacht. They had also invited a Tunisian, who boasted to me how many Jewish shops he had blown up in Tripoli. I kept my ancestry quiet, but did mention that I was about to read philosophy, and the terrorist thereafter called me a philosophist. The girls passed cherries around, the wind blew up, and soon I was prostrate on the deck, indifferent to the high risk of rolling into the sea. I told myself, in the manner of an Auschwitz inmate, that whenever in later life I felt unhappy I would look back on his moment and reflect that I had endured worse experiences. A third nauseous reminiscence: when I was a child, we went to the Scilly Isles, and one day my father took me in a boat to Black Rock. There were about twenty passengers, including a mongol who was holding a plastic windmill on a stick. Soon everyone was feeling like death and hanging over the side, except my father and the mongol, who were chatting in the back of the boat – I never found out what about.

On Wednesday I went with little Moses to a film about a youth who inexplicably strangles his girlfriend and then invites his friends to view the corpse. When I complained to M that I could not find the moral, he accused me, rightly, of tending to regard works of art as textbooks. We ate beforehand in an Indian restaurant with Judy, who was too squeamish to go to the film. Suddenly, during the meal, Moses's eyes rolled, an insane rictus distorted his face and he started breathing heavily. I feared a diabetic coma or a sex crime, and was relieved when the little chap gestured furiously at some chillies in one of the curries and fell upon the water jug. When he could concentrate again on things other than his throat, I mentioned how daunted I was by the prospect of committing all my law notes to memory, and he recommended a book called *Use Your Head*.

A moving event took place on Saturday evening: the Old Dear celebrated her seventieth birthday. After champagne at her flat, sixteen people with a high average age gathered at an up-market Chinese restaurant and ate a meal I had arranged in advance with one Mr Yow, who said, 'We loo' afta yü.' It was a jolly occasion, the decibel level increasing by the power of the number of bottles of Anjou rosé drunk. Among the guests were artists, whom the OD knows by way of my pa, and old friends from her days in UNESCO and the Wrens. Madge Leskov, with whom the OD had shared a flat in Paris in the forties, came over specially from France and was staying in the Fulham flat. Bernie Freeman, a composer, who met them both in Paris when he was studying with Milhaud and Nadia Boulanger, was also present and invited the OD, Madge and me to lunch on Sunday in the Chingford semi he inherited from his mother. Fulham to Chingford was an apoplexy-inducing journey, with Madge mindlessly reading out the names of shops and streets in her dreamy voice and the OD gasping through her teeth, hanging on to the seat and stamping on an imaginary brake pedal whenever I exceeded fifteen mph. We arrived at 2.30 p.m. and, despite my having had no breakfast, then spent three quarters of an hour drinking a bottle of champagne left over from the night before. Lunch was eventually served at teatime. The outside of Bernie's house could be used in a telly programme about Britain's housing crisis; the inside – a chaos of bric-à-brac and his mother's orthopaedic furniture – is straight from a Fritz Lang movie. Bernie has remained frozen in the Bohemianism of his Paris days (he regularly alters his date of birth in his passport). When my mother first met him, he was sharing a room with David Hamer (subsequently a successful fashion designer, subsequently dead). There was no cupboard, so they hung all their clothes on a hook on the door; it therefore required a great heave to get into the room. One day David had a guest and took all the clothes off the hook to use as a mattress for him. Bernie, returning late at night, applied the full force of his shoulder, as usual, to the door, which of course offered no resistance, so he shot across the room, falling on his face when he tipped over the sleeping guest. My mother, then an international civil servant with a large and untaxed income, was living in some style, but she nevertheless accepted an invitation to lunch chez Bernie and David, who told her to bring a knife and fork. She thought this was a joke, so they had some trouble making the cutlery go round. Bernie's early promise as a composer never led to the success he thinks he deserves. After a brief spell in the money, he has been overlooked and now grinds his teeth in jealousy of (as he calls them) Lionel

140

Fart, Andrew Lloyd Wanker, Harrison Birtwanker and Philip Glasshole. On the OD's birthday he rang up and said, 'It's your favourite composer!' 'Hallo, Lionel,' she replied, to wind him up, and then got an earful of the usual stuff about how he has more talent in his little finger than that bastard and Lloyd Wanker have between them. Bernie blames the limits of his reputation on Mrs Thatcher and consoles himself with the conviction – held on what grounds, I don't know – that he is the best-known contemporary British composer in Bulgaria.

28 November

NIPLES holds mid-sessional examinations straight after Christmas, and I am beginning to panic as I try to find time to revise on top of preparing tutorial questions. I was honoured to be asked to join an informal study group of five female students; a sixth had dropped out, and they wanted a replacement to chair discussions of criminal law (each member assuming responsibility for one subject on the syllabus). Apparently the five swots held an election and I won; I have been unable to get them to divulge my unsuccessful rivals. What my attractions are, I am not sure; perhaps they want a token boy. The other members are Shirley (the jolly fat anthropologist from Manchester), two nice girls aged about six (Annabel and Elizabeth), the domineering star pupil of the class (Barbara) and a disastrously spotty woman called Glenda. I am glad to be in charge of criminal law, which is the easiest and most interesting part of the course. This week's criminal tutorial deals with suicide pacts and abortions; there is a particularly unsavoury problem involving both, which concerns a Dr North.

*

5 December

'People who think about clothes think about food, and people who think about food don't think about anything,' says John Sessions in *The Life of Napoleon*. This aphorism worried me, for Ellénore thinks, and talks, a lot about clothes and food. Her culinary interests tend to the *cailles en sarcophage* end of the spectrum, but she displayed a sociologist's interest in English proletarian cuisine by coming to the Empire Road Gavroche for sausages, baked beans and mash. She repaid me the following night with an elaborate Thanksgiving dinner (her father was American) to which she had also invited her ma, the Old Dear, an old lady called Sibyl with a voice like Chaliapin, and a self-important poove of a curate who tried to impress with his shaky intellectual credentials. Augustus was present and told us that the Pilgrim Fathers had sailed for America on the Cauliflower. He displayed his bad upbringing by grabbing slices of turkey with his fingers as I carved; I jabbed him with the knife, but without effect. The OD was put next to the curate, called Nigel, whom she took such a dislike to that she kept her head turned away from him all evening. Ellénore's mother, who has earned my hostility by telling E that I look like Bambi, was apparently terrified of a possible second's silence and rabbited on – the other side of the bird, fortunately – about her dreary acquaintances. By the end of the evening she was drunk and, to my surprise. Ellénore announced that I would drive her home in her (the old trout's) car. E had apparently not considered my own alcohol level, the old trout's insurance policy or my return journey. She then whispered to me that I should make sure the owner-passenger got safely through the front door, as the latter had recently keeled over on the steps and knocked herself out. To my relief, *die Forelle* overheard this appendix and made a scene about not being senile yet and refusing to have that young man or anyone else see her home. The food was splendid (though my mother offended her hostess by leaving most of her chowder and all of her wild-rice-and-olive stuffing) and the washing up horrific (I managed to sever most of one finger while washing a cracked coffee jug). People who lavish five glasses on each guest should have servants.

Last weekend the Old Dear and I went up to the latifundium, a decreasingly frequent occurrence as the weather gets worse and Edie gets more demanding. The less often we go, the more guilty we feel about leaving Bird and Brenda to cope with the old idiot. Bird pays Edie more attention than she needs, and is obviously disgruntled at our failing to display the same extremes of supererogation; but this week there will probably be a lapse in the five-star standard of age concern, as Bird's son dropped dead on Sunday without warning. B's old friend Mr Shagbolt, who services our lawnmower, came round to comfort him, and the OD was indecorously amused when I suggested to her that we should ask Mr S to have a look at the bracket on the grass-box while he was there. I am so shaken by the thought of a heart attack carrying off a man not much older than me that I have given up egg sandwiches for lunch and have bought some tins of sardines and corned beef.

On Monday evening I went to the cinema with Martin Roberts, whom I had not seen since last winter. I had feared that he had ditched me as a result of a mischievous *faux pas* by Rackman. On my thirtieth birthday I gave a drinks party at the Café Italien, and on some of the invitation cards – including Rackman's but not Martin's – I wrote an additional note asking the invitee to stay to dinner. 'Have you been asked to stay to dinner?' R asked M in my presence. Martin did come for a drink, but failed to bring a present. He is a reluctant student of French literature and is writing a Ph.D. thesis on Huysmans, which he had planned to finish last February. When I asked him on Monday how it was going, he replied that he now planned to finish it next February, but, as he has written only one chapter out of eight, the prognosis is not good. Martin is one of the large number of doctoral candidates for whom the thesis becomes an incubus. He does not have many brain cells and is so sick of the whole thing that his hair is falling out, but he says that, if he failed to finish it, it would break his parents' hearts to think of the money they had wasted in supporting him all these years. His sisters are happily settled, one of them being married to a civil engineer called Bertie who works in Venezuela, the other to a truck driver in Oklahoma. Martin's father has an artificial leg and his mother has a tapeworm which makes her so tired that she spends every afternoon asleep. While she is having her four-hour nap, she leaves the phone off the hook, causing the increasingly enraged caller to think that she is merely having a conversation and that it will be worth trying again in a minute.

At Oxford Martin was a pupil of Conrad Hone, who was in love with him, and on Monday he reminded me of an incident involving Hone and some soap. Hone is an enthusiastic user of Aramis toiletries for men, and is particularly fond of the ludicrously overpriced soap-on-a-rope. While he was indulging himself with this fragrant product in one of the college showers, a loutish undergraduate Hooray Henry called Humphrey Dunton (known to his beagling and bumper-drinking cronies as Humpty Dumpty) shouted from the next cubicle, 'Hey, got any soap in there?' After considerable self-questioning, the good doctor passed his soap-on-a-rope over the partition. HD, thinking – or affecting to think – that it was college utility soap, thereupon cut it in half with a key and threw the ropeless bit back over the wall. I think it was HD who used to disrupt meetings of the college Christian Union by peeing through the keyhole.

This paragraph concerns a week's holiday that Martin, Rackman and I spent in North Wales, a depressing place, notable for rain, slate and pinched villages with grocers displaying luncheon meat beyond its Best Before date and pubs in which all the regulars start talking Welsh whenever a holidaymaker walks in. I set out, moreover, with a prejudice against the Welsh, the Old Dear having indoctrinated me since infancy with the thesis that they are devious and sex maniacs. We had booked a little house for three but, through an oversight of the Welsh Tourist Board, were allotted a cold and cavernous Victorian villa with six bedrooms, crouching under a slag heap near the dismal town of Penygroes. ('Imagine being bedridden in Penygroes,' Martin remarked.) The ostensible purpose of the holiday was to go walking, but Rackman, whose aim, it soon emerged, was to spend as much of the week as possible eating, refused to go up any mountain other than Snowdon, which has a tea shop on the summit. It is an eerie experience, having scrambled for hours through rain and fog, to hear the clink of crockery far above, and quite a relief to recuperate with a monopolistically priced Mr Kipling's cake. Rackman refused to accompany us on our other walks – 'You don't want to bust a gut,' he said, unaware of the irony – and stayed at home writing postcards. But he did join us on some motoring expeditions, including one to Portmeirion, where we coincided with an old people's coach tour from Liverpool. They were a cheery lot as they tottered round the architectural absurdities on their Zimmer frames; when Martin stumbled on some steps, an old boy chirped 'Enjoy your trip!', causing screams of merriment from the ladies with him. One evening we decided to have dinner in a hotel recommended in a guide book for its cuisine. We turned out to be the only eaters, and when we walked into the dining-room the proprietor put a Perry Como record on a portable record player in the corner. 'I'll get one of the girls to take your order,' he said forebodingly, handing us over to an unprepossessing paragon of dumb insolence. All I can remember of the food is that the smoked mackerel which I ordered for a first course had obviously just been whipped from the deep freeze, as its thicker end was crystalline and impenetrable. The rest of the time we cooked for ourselves. For one dinner Rackman, whose eyes are even bigger than his stomach, persuaded us to buy a half leg of pork, sufficient for a family of twelve. We unwisely ate it all at a sitting, and during the night we all got up at different times to be sick. When Martin and I came down, ashen-faced, in the morning, we found Rackman singing gaily over a frying pan of sausages, bacon and black pudding. The climax of his gourmandise was reached on the return journey. Martin had already left for London by car, so R and I went to Bangor for the train. We ate a cooked breakfast before setting off but, when we arrived at the station, Rackman made for the buffet, where he spent half an hour eating and drinking his elevenses. As soon as we had found seats on the train, R went along to the dining-car, leaving me with a sandwich and the Brothers Karamazov. He spent so long over his lunch that he had only been back in his seat ten minutes when the waiter walked through the carriage announcing tea. 'Fancy some tea?' Rackers asked, and led me back to his table. 'Cor, you here again, sir?' the waiter unprofessionally exclaimed, as R ordered us some toasted teacakes.

I have occasionally been on holiday by myself – not from choice, but because I have been stood up at the last minute. The weakest excuse I have received came from Jonathan, who announced that he could not join me for a walk along the Cleveland Way as someone had knocked a tennis ball into his eye. One eye would have been more than enough for some of the walk, as the Cleveland Way turned out to command a fine view of Middlesbrough. On another occasion I ended up going by myself for a week's cheap holiday in Austria. The intention had been to go in the early autumn and walk in the Alps, but there was an unwonted spasm of activity at Simpkin, so the trip had to be postponed until the end of October. By that time the Alps were shrouded in fog, and I was unable to stir from my hotel. The hotel was designed for winter sports; as in October it was almost empty, the management had decided not to put the heating on in the bedrooms, so I would linger in the deserted restaurant, listening to the musak and looking at the menu's Wimpy Bar-style colour photographs of ice cream sundaes. There was clearly no point in remaining in the mountains, so I left for Graz, where my guide book told me an arts festival called the *Steierische Herbst* was in progress. I spent the afternoon of my arrival in the city traipsing in the rain from hotel to hotel and being told every time that there was no room. Eventually, I was directed to one called Der Adler. 'Ein berühmtes Doss-Haus,' my taxi driver told me as we drove there. He was right. The hotel, over the bus station, consisted of two floors of squalid cells for the homeless. My bed creaked so much that, whenever I turned over, the dosser in the next room banged on the wall. There was no question of using the bath, as its enamel was hidden under a layer of filth. Of the lavatory I say nothing. I sought to cheer myself up with the thought of the arts festival, but it turned out that the guide book was wrong and that the *Steierische Herbst* was not beginning until the following week. The only artists who had so far arrived were a band of African drummers from Finsbury Park (curiously enough, the group with whom Hamish had lessons), so I went to a concert of theirs. I would have returned to England on the next plane, but my ticket required me to stay in Austria for a week. So I wandered round the *Sehenswürdigkeiten* in the driving rain, congratulating myself on the orange waterproof trousers I had brought for Alpine rambles. One evening I was shuffling past a concert hall which was filling with a crowd of dinner-jacketed men and mink-coated women. One lady generously pressed a ticket into my hand, so I pulled off my rubbers, expecting, from the apparent grandeur of the

147

occasion, an evening with the Vienna Philharmonic. It proved to be the local school concert; the Austrians, being provincial types, tend to overdress.

13 December

A man who has three degrees, who has published philosophical articles in journals of unparalleled learnedness, who has read *The Decline and Fall of the Roman Empire* and *A la recherche du temps perdu*, both of them unabridged and in the original, whose hobbies are learning dead languages and studying pure mathematics, and who relaxes by listening to the St Matthew Passion of Heinrich Schütz, is unlikely to enjoy a Christmas party in a Porsche showroom, but that is what Ellénore asked me to accompany her to on Tuesday evening. I had assumed that half the revellers would be oily men in green overalls and the other half city types with braying voices and broadly striped shirts. In fact only the EC2 brigade were there, many of them unaccompanied and leering at anything with a Gucci handbag. The occasion was graced by Dr Wolfgang Porsche (or 'Wolfi'), an elderly man who gave a speech in which he expressed regret at being unable to know all his customers personally and said how glad he was to be at the showroom tonight – where, he might have added, he would be less likely to meet a client than to have champagne poured over his shirt front by one of the bibulous coterie of the garage manager's wife. Wolfi was invisible throughout his speech, as he stood in the centre of a circle of dazedly admiring men and women, all taller than he. There were few cars in sight, but tables groaning with drink stood at intervals of six feet, from which Ellénore made me serve her frequently. I had hoped she would at least satisfy my anthropologist's interest by introducing me to people, but in fact most of her circle had been dropped from the list of invitees, having drunkenly disgraced themselves last year, and I met only a taciturn and hostile lout who looked like Nigel Lawson after an hour on the rack.

Little Augustus had been whipped off for the night by Granny, who did not want him to see his mother drunk, so we were able to lie in, which was good for my beloved, who has a heavy cold. I am an oasis of radiant health: E can hardly breathe and has a voice three octaves deeper than usual, Jow-enn is coughing like a donkey, NIPLES sounds like the terminal ward of the Brompton Chest Hospital, Ike Van Pelt – the husband of one of the Old Dear's chums – was found yesterday morning lying on the pavement outside Hyde Park, having dropped dead while jogging, and Augustus has been consorting with a child who has mumps. If Augustus has caught it, he will start to swell on Christmas Day, the day before he is going on holiday to China with his mother and grandmother. Having had no childhood diseases as a child, and only one since (v. 27 June), I am panic-stricken, for the possible consequences of a grown man's getting mumps are well known: inflamed testicles carried before you in a wheelbarrow, permanent impotence and withering of the male member. Rackman, who has likewise escaped the disease hitherto, is equally worried, though he observed that his member could not shrivel any further – a proposition that I, sadly, am in a position to confirm. I might also have consoled him by pointing out 'hat, since he has a neck like a Prussian Junker and jowls like the Godfather, any swelling of his parotid glands would be unobservable. I phoned my doctor, a kindly and incompetent fairy called Larry, to ask whether I should have an injection or whether by now the horse would have bolted, but he seemed not to understand the question and told me to do nothing unless Augustus himself becomes mumpish. I don't trust Larry, for he has never cured me of anything. The Bedrich Smetana of Catford, I have suffered for years from deafness and tinnitus in the left ear and, when recently the condition worsened, I asked him if something could be done. Anyone with a bottom-grade GCSE in biology knows that most of the ear is invisible from the outside, but Larry, having given me a hearing test which confirmed that I was deaf as a post, peered into my ear, saw nothing but a bit of wax, and pronounced that I was a freak of nature and had to live with it.

I have met with equally dismissive unconcern for the fact that I see double. An expensive consultant ophthalmologist told me the trouble was in my brain, leaving me wondering whether I had a neurophysiological disorder or whether he thought I was a hypochondriac. I therefore persuaded an amiable fat girl called Monica, with whom I had a two-night stand at Oxford, to ask her father, an eye surgeon, to arrange for me to be examined at Moorfields. When I arrived the nurse had no record of the appointment but said she would squeeze me in nevertheless. It turned out that I had come during the surgery for visually disturbed children, and I was shown into a nursery where the other patients – average age eighteen months – crawled around the floor, squinting at soft toys. Eventually I was placed in a tiny chair and given an eye test designed for the very young. 'Look through these glasses,' the nurse coaxed in a *Listen With Mother* voice, 'and tell me if you can see the birdie fly away from the little red sheep.' After this humiliation, I was led into a room where a board of specialists glared at me across the table. Their spokesman, a Hungarian, told me severely in broken English that I was *not* seeing double and could therefore go home. The last time I saw Monica was when I took the Old Dear to the cinema for a birthday treat, and M was the usherette who showed us to our seats.

I must withdraw my earlier remark about being in fine health, for, not only are my sense organs in disarray, I also have one leg longer than the other. I first became aware of this as a child, and thereupon limped around until I forgot about it. My mother's uncle Frank sought to

150

console me by saying that, even if one leg was an inch longer than the other, the second leg compensated by being an inch shorter, but I was too distraught to find this funny. My left leg, which I took to be the longer one, is in fact the shorter, as is revealed (a) by the fact that the left leg of new pairs of trousers always has to be turned up more than the right and (b) by the angle of my hips when I stand naked in front of the mirror.

22 December

When I left Simpkin it was agreed, first, that I would not have a corporeal present but be given money instead and, second, that my farwell party would be postponed until the autumn; but Old Simpkin, by conflating these propositions, arrived at the conviction that I did not want a party at all. Clearly *he* did not want one, fearing perhaps that, like the last time, I would soon be scurrying back to the leisurely security of secondhand bookselling – in which case festivities would have been a waste of money. When the leaves had all fallen from the trees and frost lay on the ground, I told Louise to give the old boy a nudge, which she did twice, but each time he repeated that I did not want a party and then went on about the low level of profits. She finally persuaded him to organize a dinner, but without convincing him that he had been wrong. Judging by his surliness on the happy occasion, he clearly thought that I had been difficult and changed my mind. A group of us went to a new Siamese restaurant called the Bahn Thai (which Old S implausibly suggested meant 'the way to Thailand') and ate a lavish red and green dinner, over which Old S told me that Tessa Plumptre – who has an enormous voice and walks about in a crash helmet – had recently had her feet filleted. She was brought up in China and her parents entrusted her to a native nurse who – presumably without the parents' knowledge – bound Tessa's feet in the traditional manner. As a result T has never been able to walk more than a hundred yards, so, to increase her range, she went into hospital a couple of months ago, where the bones of her feet were replaced with bits of Meccano. Presumably she now has to be careful not to walk near magnets. The conversation then moved to a legal case involving seamless sausages, and from there to two shrunken heads that are soon to be sold at Christies. They are of particular interest because (i) they are European and (ii) it is known whom they belonged to – Herr & Frau Doktor something-or-other, a couple of German missionaries. Someone asked how heads are shrunk, and we agreed that they must be boned, like a chicken; I suggested that they were then soaked overnight in Ariel Automatic. At this point little Moses, who had already gone pale during the story about the filleted feet, pleaded with us to stop, so we talked instead about Manik, Simpkin's Indian cleaner, whose proudest boast is that he owns half a bus in Calcutta, which he intends to trade in for a house.

Friday was the last day of term at NIPLES and, as Mr Taylor (constitutional law) was leaving, Shirley proposed that we surprise him with drinks and something to eat at the end of his final lecture. Students better disposed than I towards the appalling Taylor produced crisps and warm white wine from their briefcases, and I guiltily nibbled one of several formless sponges that Shirley had baked. They had been intended to be rock cakes, but S had been distracted while making them by a neighbour who had dropped in to complain that her husband was a manic-depressive-paranoid-schizophrenic. Shirley tried to assure her that he was unlikely to be all these things, but she was unconsoled. The party became alcoholically merry and some people became embarrassingly confidential. Glenda – the student with incandescent acne – told me she was a lesbian and proud of it (she perhaps is responsible for channelling the Institute's social fund into the dirndl pockets of the Lesbian Society) and a girl called Becky, who has a squeaky voice and commutes from Southend, gave me her phone number and told me she admired me for having a pee each day (presumably trying to refer to my doctorate). The drinks had a destabilizing influence on the meeting, directly afterwards, of the swot group. Glenda fell asleep and the other four women spent some time discussing Richard Bennett (single-handed lecturer on the law of trusts), who it turns out is regarded by most female students as a sex object. Barbara, as usual, let us know her high opinion of herself and broke into Greek and Latin on the shakiest of pretexts. 'Ergo,' she proclaimed in her overbearing voice, and then helpfully added 'therefore'; 'Thank you,' I interjected, and got a dirty look. Barbara speaks Latin as if it were Italian, to show that she is au courant with the current state of research into phonetic history. Having read Greats at Oxford, she was made to dabble in ancient philosophy and was recently kind enough to give me her solution to the paradox of the heap. She has a confident opinion on every topic, announcing always, 'This happens to be something I know rather a lot about.'

That evening I went to a house-warming-cum-thirtieth-birthday party given by Milo Darwin, a distantish friend from Oxford. He is an undeservedly agreeable lout who does a bit of painting and a bit of journalism. The Old Dear once set eyes on him when he came to a party of mine, and she drew me aside, exclaiming, 'Who is that evil man?' When I asked her why she thought he was evil, she hissed, 'He isn't wearing any socks!' The flat he was warming is a flimsy conversion; I made a dent in the wall when I leaned against it. The party was full of Oxford acquaintances, but I recognized hardly any of them. I glared at a woman who was sitting by the drinks table giving suck to a child, and when she caught my eye she beamed and cried, 'Joe!' Hurriedly converting the scowl into a noncommittal grin, I asked her what she was up to these days, hoping this might give me a clue as to who she was, but the only memory her prattle raked up in me was that she had got a third in Arabic. 'Didn't you read Arabic?' I asked chirpily. 'How clever of you to remember!' I was saved from further embarrassment by having to set off for Catford. At midnight London Bridge station, where I was to change from tube to big train, was more crowded than it usually is in the rush hour, and almost everyone was drunk, having been to an office party. Being unable to get on the first five trains, I went to look for a taxi, but an ugly scene was developing at the rank as paper-hatted typists shouted 'Fuck yourself' to stockbrokers who were braying 'Hey!' at them for queue jumping. I managed to squeeze into the last train of the evening and enjoyed a concentrate of Dickens and Breughel as passengers threw up out of the windows and over each other's shoes. Having got out at Lewisham (the nearest the train would take me to home) I saw in the corner of my eye a fist fly from one of the train windows and knock a disagreeable-looking hulk with Doc Martens and an earring across the platform. With some reason, he rushed into the train, and thuds and screams could be heard inside. He finally emerged, bloodier than before, shouting, 'If I see you again, you're dead!' The train started to move and some girls in the carriage shouted 'Bye bye' to him in jeering voices, while he shook his fist and yelled 'Fuck yourself', a popular expression on Network SouthEast at Christmas.

As a result of Rackman's rent increase, Jow-enn is unable to go away for Christmas Day, and relations between them are at their nadir. R has taken to harassing her by crashing around outside her room at 1.00 a.m., so she has moved up to the garret that in happier days was occupied by dear old Leslie. The electric socket in the garret is dicey, so Jojo asked her landlord to check it. While she was out, he tested it by plugging in her ghetto blaster, and a cajoling American voice came out of the loudspeaker saying, 'Now clench your buttocks.' Rackman switched off in horror, and looked sceptical when J told him that it was her relaxation tape. I am now tormented by an image of Jow-enn trying to relax by digging her fingers into her bum. The other evening, when she and I were having dinner alone in the kitchen, I told her that Rackman was a transvestite. She started, her mug of hot water pressed, unsipped, to her lips, and sat rigid as I made up a story about his spending weekends at a transvestite hotel in Bromley. Eventually she murmured, 'This needs a lot of digesting,' and pushed her Marks and Spencer coleslaw round the plate, lost in anxious speculation. 'So don't be surprised if you catch him in stilettos and a tutu,' I said breezily, but then thought the joke had gone far enough and tried to convince her that I had been having her on. She was not wholly reassured, for the story is not implausible; as she said at the time, there's something fishy about Rackman. He and I went for a walk in the park on Saturday, and I was reminded of the Baron de Charlus as I watched him gazing intently at one of the implements in the exercise area – a row of rings and chains suspended from an overhead beam. Rackman was delighted when I told him about the transvestite yarn, and promised to convince Jow-enn of some even more lurid story about me. He hates her so much that he forbade me to ask her to join the small dinner party that was to take place at the Empire Road Athenaeum on Saturday evening. I kindheartedly invited her nevertheless, but the gloom of the house seemed to have got to her, for she declined, saying she didn't feel like spending the evening talking sweet nothings. I was offended that she thought sweet nothings would be appropriate, and shall not invite her to anything again.

The guest we asked first was Mary, but we then thought she would like someone as well as us to talk to. 'Why not ask your friend Colin?' I said as a joke, for Colin, a lodger in Rackman's old flat, is a spindly and autistic accountant with a skin disease. It was a foolish remark, for, as Colin really is a friend of Rackman's, the latter did not see the joke and invited him. Mary has just been to deliver some seaweed to Hamish in Hamburg and was irritated, having recently sent him a stroboscope (v. 14 November), to find that he already has a much bigger one there, which he stares into for relaxation in the way that Jow-enn clenches her buttocks. M told us how, when she and Hamish were married, she went into the bedroom one day to find that he had erected a large wooden pyramidal frame over the bed, with a small copper pyramid perched on the top. Its purpose, according to Hamish, was to focus some special rays on to the bed which would give them a more satisfying night's sleep. Mary did not find it had this effect: apparently it was hard to get into the bed at all with the pyramid there, and she kept banging her knee on it during the night. She is spending Christmas with her sister, who, the reader will remember, is married to a man forty years older than herself and has two dogs, one of which is epileptic. Her sister does not have a spare room, so last Christmas Mary slept in a sleeping bag on the sofa. While she was asleep, Punch, the epileptic dog, slid in beside her and woke her by having an attack of *grand mal* in the bag – legs kicking, jaws snapping and mouth frothing. Bess, the other dog, is upset by Punch's turns, and bites him to try and make him pull himself together. As a result P is missing half an ear.

29 December

The festive season ended with the Old Dear's screaming 'I'll kill you!' at Edie and my throwing some crockery at a wall in a rage. I can't remember why I threw the crockery, but the OD's outburst was due to some nonsense about Edie's cat, Lupin, which E keeps denying is hers.

The OD found her tottering up our garden path with Lupin in her arms and saying, nodding at our house, 'I think he must belong to the people who live there; but they seem to be away.' Paranoia is now setting in: Edie hides things – the cleaning lady recently discovered a bowl of fruit in the wardrobe – and then can't find them, and then accuses 'people' of having pinched them. Alarming sexual fantasies are also developing. 'Don't go in there!' she cried to the OD, pointing to her bedroom, 'there are men in there; they've been there all night.' Mr Bird, when he heard about this, uncharacteristically retorted, 'She should be so lucky!' These utterances of Edie's are at the perspicuous end of her spectrum; much of the time she burbles a semantic and syntactic chaos that is as hard to imitate as it is to generate a sequence of random numbers. Before she dies I intend to make a tape of one of her monologues, transcribe it, present it as my own work and be acclaimed as the new Beckett.

Until the explosive finale, the Old Dear and I maintained an unstable equilibrium, largely explained by my locking myself in my study to read *Barnaby Rudge*. The reader will recall that a couple of Xmases ago the OD invited to lunch a man with terminal cancer and his family. This year she asked his widow (Winnie) and only child (Julia). Winnie is an almost perfect sphere – a terrifying sight in trousers – and wheezes desperately after walking a couple of paces. Julia, who is in her early thirties, is tall, bony, spotty and difficult. I was consoled to find that her behaviour towards her mother exhibits an even more extreme oscillation between frenzied irritation and guilt-ridden affection than mine does towards the Old Dear: she spent most of the weekend abusing poor Winnie, but showered her with presents bearing effusive labels. In my view the blessings of giving are overrated, and I have always preferred to receive – though I am not much interested in either. I was pleased, however, to be given various Latin texts by Rackman and the OD, who also – managing for once, in an access of yuletide spirit, to restrain herself from idiotically telling me that I have enough books already – produced an *Oxford Companion to German Literature*. I usually leave Christmas shopping so late that the shops are otherwise deserted, but this year my timing was awry and I spent an alienating morning being squashed and enraged. My route descended the scale of retailing prestige, beginning in the Harrods perfumery and passing, by way of the Reject Shop – from which I was driven by a continuous loop of carols in a jazz version sung by a downmarket Ella Fitzgerald with a big band – to a scene of bedlam in the Catford W.H. Smith, where I bought a box of Luxury Grade crackers which we forgot to pull.

My indifference to the Kula ring irritated Ellénore's mamma, an incorrigible ritualist, but the gravamen of her hostility towards me is that I am penniless. 'You need someone to look after you,' she recently told her daughter. A title might have placated her, but it is too late for me to start pretending that my father's was hereditary and that I have no older brother. I have done as much as I can to endear myself by acting as *sommelier* at an uninteresting cocktail party given by the old trout, though my kind intentions misfired when her cousin Raoul strolled off while I was pouring champagne into his glass, leaving me emptying the bottle over a Persian carpet. When I shrieked, Raoul turned and asked acidulously, 'Was that my fault or yours?' Raoul is a *distingué* Frenchman in his sixties, and his only topics of conversation are his connections and his money. He numbed me with a monologue about his dinners with the Comte de Paris and some friends of his who used to own all the Pyrenees but now, poor things, only have a valley left, and I almost choked on my prune-wrapped-in-bacon when he recollected how his wife's eye had fallen out when he crashed his Lamborghini while trying to make it go faster than 150 mph. The point of this anecdote was to impress me with the fact that, having written the car off, the first thing he did (before calling an ambulance for the unwilling cyclops in the passenger seat) was to order a new one. At the end of the party the small group remaining sat about comparing plays they had seen, and Ellénore almost ended our relationship by announcing that she had been to *Amadeus* six times. Her brow is regrettably unMahlerian: she thinks that *Pilgrim's Progress* and *The Thirty-Nine Steps* were written by the same person and, when I demanded an explanation of the two Barry Manilow LPs in her box of records, she said unconvincingly, 'They were left here by my ex-husband.' 'How could you marry a man who listens to B. Manilow?' I retorted. 'He didn't listen to him when we got married,' E said, leaving me to conclude that she must have driven him to it. Among the other apostles of high culture at the party was an astrologer called Inga who, whenever she referred to a star of the stage, would use their Christian name. 'Maggie was *so* powerful in *Coming In To Land*,' she drawled, despite never having met Miss Smith in her life. Inga went on to let us know how wealthy she was by telling us of all the jewellery she had had stolen. 'I'm not replacing it,' she declared, 'from now on I'm putting all my money in houses.' 'Well, there's nothing more fun than houses!' was the baffling reply of Ellénore's Aunt Edith, an old lady who was clearly once formidable but now has a tendency to ramble; she went on to embarrass the company by recollecting a production at the Santa Fé opera in which a singer had her pubic hair combed on stage. Aunt Edith, Ellénore's mother, E and the two boys have now gone to China, leaving me in E's flat to look after Gridley, who, apart from being insecure emotionally, has a broken leg as a result of leaping at the Christmas tree. Before leaving, E's elder son gave me his gastric flu, which I am only distracted from by a mountain of revision for the law exams. My bowels have been delicate since Christmas Day, when a fart got out of control and I shat myself. Fortunately I was in my bedroom, so I tore my trousers

159

and pants off and rushed into the bathroom, heedless of the risk of meeting Winnie or Julia on the landing and their seeing brown drips on my calves. Some liquid faecal matter had also sprayed on to the bedroom carpet and, the carpet itself being brown, I was unsure that my frenzied wiping of it with lavatory paper was effective.

5 January

Derek Badham left a phone message with Jow-enn asking me to dinner. The note she left me said that I was to take £5 and a bottle of wine, which enraged me, for Badham is a man of boundless wealth, but I then decided it must be a charity do. In fact it was his birthday, and the remark about the dosh and the drink had been a prank: Badham explained that, whenever he hears an Australian accent, he recognizes the potential victim of a practical joke. But, since in this case the Australian was just a conduit pipe and the joke was unamusing, the message was misconceived. He was however delighted to have his theory about Australians confirmed when I told him the transvestism story. Diana Radcliffe, formerly of King's College and now a serf in the Murdoch empire, was at the birthday party, avoiding the estimable Abram and Samantha (for the reason, v. 6 June), and I also met an Irish psychiatrist and her husband, a man with a packaging business. Having a nose for an infinite regress, I asked him whether he supplied his packaging materials in a package and, if so, who supplied that package; but he didn't see what I was driving at, and replied that it came from Hong Kong. I was so proud of my quip that I told the Old Dear about it, but she remarked drily that the man must have thought I was a complete idiot. She is being tormented by phone calls that are abusive by default: when she lifts the receiver, there is silence the other end. Thinking that the troublemaker is likely to be deterred by a masculine voice, the OD now answers the phone with a hello worthy of Monostatos and, if you don't speak within the next nanosecond, starts telling you in her new gravelly voice that the call is being monitored by the Metropolitan Police.

I accepted an invitation from Abram to Samantha's for New Year's Eve, but, since it emerged that the celebration was to consist in the three of us going Dutch in her local Chinese, and that we should have to sit next to the fish tank as her thirteen-year-old son Theodore, an icthyophile, would be joining us, I accepted a later invitation, telling Abram at the last minute that my gastric condition had plummeted and that I would be bound to vomit over the Char Sui. The other invitation was from Campaspe Walters, whom I barely know; she had been feeding Gridley before I took over, and left a note on the table in Ellénore's flat. On the evening of the 31st, Campaspe rang up, perplexingly, to ask me my name and to tell me that one of the other guests had recently been widowed. It seems that for some reason Campaspe thought I was likely to make wisecracks about death, but her warning failed to take counter-suggestibility into account. I once went to visit a lady whose husband had just died from what they call a 'massive coronary', and kept telling myself on the way not to mention hearts or death. A friend of mine was there, we started fooling about, and the widow said, 'You two are like Morecambe and Wise.' 'Yes,' I replied merrily, remembering the sad end of Eric and Ernie's act, 'one of us will have a heart-attack in a minute.' The New Year's Eve widow was one of two women at the party called Joy, and I could never remember which one I was supposed to be gentle with. There were also present a female art historian, who looked at me with what Rebecca used to call bedroom eyes, and a Conservative MP called Hubert with a camp manner and a voice so loud that he managed to take the credit for my witty remarks to my neighbour by repeating them to the company at large. Someone made the

161

profound observation that it was a sign of the high level of unemployment that one now saw Brussels sprouts being picked not by wizened dodderers but by sprightly young men. I suggested to bedroom eyes that picking sprouts might turn sprightly, or sproutly, young men into dodderers. 'Ah ha, sproutly young men!' bawled Hubert, and the party collapsed with mirth. He has also to answer for the fact that at 1.30 a.m. he produced from his pocket a quiz to sustain the flagging conversation. Nobody chez Walters seemed to have enjoyed the last year, and they glared at me when I declared that it had been one of the most enjoyable of my life.

Matthew Lettin, a monster of self-satisfaction and smart-aleckery, is an astrophysicist I met at Makreel. He drifts around American universities – the graduate schools' deplorable answer to Groucho Marx – and comes home to England every Christmas, when he tries to look me up. I thought that this year I had avoided an evening of his whinnying laugh by hiding in Ellénore's flat with Gridley, but Lettin traced the phone number and arranged to meet me for dinner on New Year's Day. Even then I almost escaped, as the door bell had broken, but, having failed to get a reply, he went to a phone box and rang up, demanding to be let in. He told me he had a stomach ulcer, so I took him to an Indian restaurant. There his prattle unwontedly dried up, partly perhaps as a result of acute gastric pain, partly because, while talking about his Ph.D. thesis, he realized with shock that he could not remember any of the books in its bibliography. I sympathized, vainly trying as I am to swot up law notes for the New Year exams next week. I stare at them for hours every day, and facts of cases, their names and the principles they instantiate float about my brain, but without connection. Gridley loyally sits under the desk all day, untying my shoe laces. To make up for his recent period of immobility, he now climbs into the bed with me at night and tears around under the clothes, bleating, at 4 a.m. He enchanted Sara, who came to dinner with Neville on Saturday. It was a tiring evening as, the door bell being dead, I had instructed the guests to shout or hoot when they arrived and therefore had to run down four flights of stairs whenever I heard a noise in the street. Neville and Sara have just bought a terraced house in Cockfosters and over dinner told us about their neigbour, a deranged man of fifty-nine, who had lived there all his life with his mother until she died last year; they hear him now through the party wall running around the house all night, mumbling, 'Jesus fucking Christ, Christ fucking Jesus, fucking Jesus Christ.' People who live in areas as remote as that deserve such neighbours, I remarked to Rackman, who was present. Neville appeared to have brain damage or to be on amphetamines, as during the evening his conversation became slower and slower, crumbling by the dessert into aposiopesis. Mary joined us halfway through the meal, having just played a concert round the corner at the Albert Hall. She told us that, to be kind to her hamster, she had put up a poster of Aleppo above its cage; apparently all British hamsters are descended from one that was imported from Aleppo in 1837. She also revealed more of the mysteries of Hamish's secret cupboard. The latest of its contents that he has asked her to send him is a meter for monitoring his brain waves – an item that I had always thought so sophisticated technologically as to be found only in the neurophysiological wards of teaching hospitals. Hamish's interest in brain waves stems from a visit he made to a club of brain enthusiasts, who discovered that his brain was emitting an unusually high level of alpha waves. This meant, apparently, that he was clinically asleep.

*

16 January

Having learned at my mother's knee to touchtype, I paid
off my debts of crapulence on coming down from Oxford
by working as an Alfred Marks girl. The ladies in Alfred
Marks are ingratiating and address you by your Christian name without permission, but turn hard-nosed and
tight-lipped if you impugn their tax deductions. The first
place they sent me was the Confidential Duplicating
Department of the Independent Broadcasting Authority,
where I shared a pool, or puddle, with two divorcees in
their forties, Mavis and Moira. The typing work was
sporadic, so I managed to read *Don Quixote, Heart of
Darkness*, Vasari's *Lives*, Leavis's *The Living Principle*,
Mill's autobiography and *Pilote de guerre* against the
background of M's and M's prattle. Moira, who kept
resolving to leave, was always affronted by something
or other and would complain to Mavis that so-and-so
was 'so rude' (which she pronounced 'rewd'). Once the
monotony was broken by a woman coming in with a
questionnaire. 'Now, girls,' she began, to my irritation,
'we want your opinion on telly advertisements for femi-
nine hygiene.' The question was whether it was accept-
able for tampons to appear on the screen or whether
such advertisements should be restricted to pictures of
smiling women indulging in vigorous activities. 'Well,
my opinion is . . .' I started, but was cut off with 'No, just
the girls, thank you.' While Mavis and Moira hummed
and hahd, the lady went on, 'We're giving the new
advertisements a trial period.' I guffawed, but my colleagues showed not a flicker, being either slower-witted
or more grown up than I. In the next room the
duplicating machine was operated by a youth called
Ron, who had to take one morning off to testify at
Willesden Crown Court, having been to a jovial party at
which a guest had cut off one of the host's fingers with a
penknife. My performance at the IBA was so outstanding that they kept me for eight weeks and then

offered me a permanent job, which I declined.

I have held more transient posts in the accounts department of the Economist Intelligence Unit, where a woman came up and asked me if I was Miss Smith; at the NFU, where I had to type the President's thank-you letters for donations to a disaster fund; at Bowater Scott, where I sat next to a glass display case containing different types of lavatory paper; and at Morgan Guaranty, where I was put off a banking career by the sight of obviously high-ranking employees, with grey hair and distinguished faces, sitting at rows of desks as if they were taking an exam. There I was made to share a table with a woman who moronically sucked boiled sweets all day; I wanted to kill her. My shortest job was a morning as a telex operator for a Pakistani shipping company consisting of father, son, one other darky and a heap of lever-arch files in one room of a flat in Bayswater. The father spent most of the time on a kidney machine installed in the next room; he looked as if he were sitting in a dentist's chair. Occasionally he would emerge to dictate a telex with his sleeve rolled up and a six-inch pipe sticking out of his arm; the pipe contained a thin yellow liquid which was prevented from squirting over my keyboard by a dainty tap. I was sacked at lunchtime for not having the faintest idea how a telex machine worked.

The most depressing job was in the Ombudsman's office. The corridors smelled of disinfectant, the walls were civil service green and the lighting was flickering fluorescent. I shared a room with four teenage girls, all of them ESN. One of them, Lisa (pronounced 'Leessa'), had in addition a cleft palate, for which she was victimized by her colleagues. Like the lady in Morgan Guaranty, she kept a store of boiled sweets in her drawer, and one day, before she arrived, the other girls hid them. When Leessa discovered she had nothing to roll around her king-size oral cavity, she started to sob. The others managed to grasp that their hilarious joke had gone too far, but were too ashamed to admit that they had nicked the sweets. I had to type reports by the Ombudsman in reply to letters, of complaint about negligent medical treatment. The letters, often illiterate scrawls on scraps of paper, contained heartbreaking stories of babies being blinded with excessive oxygen, of tonsillectomies resulting in paralysis and of legs being amputated in error. The Ombudsman would hypnotize the victims with orotund screeds in which the words 'appropriate' and 'inappropriate' did duty for all the more usual terms of moral approbation and disapprobation like 'right' and 'wrong'. 'The hospital has apologized,' he wrote to a woman whose child had been turned into a vegetable (she did not say what kind) by a newly qualified doctor, 'and I am of opinion, taking all the circumstances into account, that this is the appropriate response.' Work was interrupted one afternoon by the explosion, a few yards down the road, of the bomb that did for Airey Neave; my colleagues, not satiated by the stomach-churning material in their typewriters, spent some hours pressed to the window in the hope of seeing something horrific.

I have just finished the New Year examinations at the Institute, an enervating climax to several weeks' staring at files of notes. While revising, I assumed an intense expression in the hope that this would help the material go in, and managed to absorb one or two facts, for instance that 'grievous bodily harm' was pronounced by the Lord Chancellor in the case of *DPP v Smith* to mean 'really serious bodily harm,' while in a later case the learned judge ruled that the 'really' was unnecessary and that GBH was in fact 'serious bodily harm.' Last Sunday, the day before the exams began, my swot group assembled in Glenda's flat, where we played Tortious Pursuit; this game, invented by Shirley, is identical to Trivial Pursuit, except that the players ask each other about legal cases. Glenda's landlord, a lawyer, sat in the corner of the room throughout and must have been enraged by our garblings. Seeing the law as a stepping-stone to boundless wealth, I was dismayed by the squalor of the flat, but apparently he does Legal Aid work. Since, however, he specializes in housing cases, I should have thought he could do better for himself. The place was strewn with defunct consumer durables, the bathroom containing two washing machines, only one of which worked – you had to climb over the other in order to have a pee. The area was filled to pavement level with scrap metal; when he decides that a cooker or a fridge or a telly is beyond repair, he tosses it out there in the hope that the dustmen will collect it (which they won't).

Sitting exams is a barely tolerable strain for a man of my years, though I did manage to keep my seat; a dim girl called Kath swept from the examination hall ten minutes into the trusts paper, having been overwhelmed by the possibility of a completely constituted trust of the benefit of a covenant, and a highly strung man fell from his chair with a thud and was dragged from the room, like a figure from *Journey's End*, over the invigilator's shoulder. It was dispiriting to see how fast the woman next to me wrote, but consoling to see that the ten lines she got down in the time it took me to dot an i consisted of waffle like, 'On the other hand, as regards the defendant, it might conceivably be objected on the plaintiff's behalf that. . .'. I shall be surprised if I fail and surprised if the examiners see in my answers a budding Lord Denning. Only in the land law paper was I aware of writing utter drivel, and I am reasonably confident about my answers to the criminal questions. One of these again contained a couple of characters called Don and Vic, and it was hard to keep in mind that this time Don was not a man of low intelligence (v. 8 November). The question went like this: 'Don has a history of chronic alcoholism, but has recently managed to give up drinking, having joined a local branch of Alcoholics Anonymous. One evening he arrives home from a meeting of the group to find his wife, Wendy, in bed with Vic. Vic says, "You might as well go back to your boozy pals, Wendy's had enough of living with an old soak like you." Don then flies into a rage, seizes a bedside lamp and hits Vic over the head with it, cutting him badly. Wendy, in terror, jumps out of the bedroom window and is killed when she is impaled on some railings below. Don, full of remorse, calls an ambulance and Vic is taken to hospital where he dies two days later, having been given an antibiotic to which he is dangerously allergic. Consider Don's liability for the deaths of Vic and Wendy.' I also answered questions on suicide pacts, bigamy and sexual intercourse with young girls.

Ellénore and family are back from China with photographs of themselves peering over the Great Wall and pretending to be emperors in the Forbidden City. I unwisely spent the night after their return in their flat, with the result that I was woken at 3.00 a.m. by the nippers, who were still on Peking time. I spent the rest of the day – my birthday – feeling like death and resolving to resume the role of arch-hierophant of the New Chastity, but have since mellowed, having spent an enjoyable evening with my beloved at *L'Italiana in Algeri*. Anyone who had heard no music but that of Rossini would agree with Stravinsky's claim that music has nothing to do with the expression of emotion.

Stop press from the geriatric ward: this morning the Old Dear went round to Edie's and found in the bedroom the customary kitchen bowl of urine and the human turds in Lupin's litter tray. 'Why don't you use the lavatory!' the OD exploded. 'Lavatory?' Edie replied vaguely. 'Come with me,' the OD barked, dragging Edie into the bathroom. 'You see this?' she said, pointing at the jakes. 'Well, you sit on it, like this,' (giving a demonstration) 'then you do what you have to do, and then you FLUSH!' – giving a massive tug at the handle and imagining it was

Edie's nose. 'Ah yes,' E responded dreamily, but she is no longer educable and the OD intends to drive to Chelmsford, where they sell a special Elsan for the old and infirm to have in the bedroom. I fear this will make the situation worse, for I recently talked to a woman whose senile mother-in-law, when reminded of the lavatory, started washing her hands in it. That is harmless enough in the case of an ordinary WC, but if Edie does the same with the Elsan she will cover her hands in chemicals and worse.

25 January

When I went round to the Old Dear's recently, I found Winkle (the larger and more pudding-like of her cats) crouching miserably under the chair with a hideous swelling behind his ear that made him look like the Elephant Man. The OD blamed it on Nicky, an immense and ungenerous black tom, named on account of the nicks he takes out of neighbouring cats' ears. Nicky lives with Brenda Runeckles, Bird's amour, who snapped that N could not possibly have been responsible either for the swelling or for the serrated edge that poor Winkle's ear developed at the same time, and Bird toadyishly chimed in that W must have been bitten by a rat. Bird clearly thought that Winkle had suffered no more than he deserved, for W terrorizes B's little female cat, Bimbo, and recently caused her similar aural damage. Mr Lush, the vet, has prescribed antibiotics and ear drops for Winkle. The Old Dear was able to cozen W into taking the pills by crushing them and wrapping them in liver, but needed another pair of hands for the drops. I wrapped W in a towel, leaving just his head sticking out, so that he looked like a baby, and held him in a vice-like grip while the OD squeezed the viscous yellow liquid into the infected ear. Mr Lush had told her then to stroke behind the ear and wait for a gurgling noise, but she stroked too vigorously, causing the swelling to burst and pus to well up. Winkle did not like this at all, and shook his head violently, sending a shower of mixed pus and drops into the faces of his incompetent surgeons. 'Poor little pussy,' I muttered feebly, remembering Rackman's quip.

It has been a week of nasty bodily events. Shirley turned up at the Institute on Monday saying that her insides had fallen out over the weekend, apparently a frequent occurrence with her. Various girls then clustered round and conspiratorially whispered words like 'Feminax', so I withdrew and do not know the details. But S sat next to me in the lecture, which alarmed me, for, being so large, she must have a lot of insides to come out; a relapse would have ruined my briefcase. And then there are Rackman's testicles. A year ago R went to the doctor with painful balls and, the reader will remember, was told to wear boxer shorts. Twelve months with a free-swinging scrotum failed to alleviate the trouble, and Rackman – as a result, I suspect, of browsing in medical dictionaries – is now convinced that he has varicose veins in his left testis. He went to the Nuffield Clinic, where an Indian put a finger up his arse and then told R to ask the receptionist for a semen-sample bottle. Poor Rackman, having stammered out the request with glowing cheeks, told the girl he would bring the sample along the following day. 'Oh no, you must provide it now,' she replied crisply, 'It only stays fresh a couple of hours.' And she packed him off to the gents without even giving him a girlie magazine. I don't know what a bottle for semen looks like; it can't have a narrow neck, or there would be a problem in aiming. The next stage in Rackman's treatment is an ultrasound bath, whatever that is; R perhaps lies in the bath while nurses blow dog-whistles at his genitals. I hope this is not done at Empire Road.

For once I had a quiet week, spending most evenings alone, reading and doing my Latin lessons. On Monday, however, I went with Ellénore to the cinema. As I was buying the Maltesers I bumped into Rupert Hoare, who cried 'Hellay' and asked me whether I was going to see the film or had just come into the cinema to get warm. On Saturday evening Ellénore graciously allowed me to use her flat for a drinks party to celebrate my being thirty-one years, two weeks and one day – an important age in a man's life. She made fancy things on sticks and I provided the guests with a choice of white wine, orange juice or white wine, keeping a Scotch for myself in the kitchen. Many of the guests, being peasants, seemed to think that a drinks party lasts all evening, so at 9.30 p.m. I had to turf them out in order to go to dinner with a select few. The difficulty was to separate the diners from the riff-raff. After some whispering, I managed to send the former to the appointed restaurant, murmuring that Ellénore and I would join them as soon as we had got rid of the *canaille*. 'Thank you so much; see you again soon, I hope!' the members of the cenacle hammed, winking ludicrously, as they set off. Unfortunately I had forgotten to whisper to Louise, whom I had previously told to stay, so she started to leave, looking crestfallen, with Moses and Judy. The simplest thing would have been to invite M and J to dinner as well, but Ellénore had drawn me aside during the party and demanded an explanation of 'that appalling little man with a dirty neck, who has the nerve to come to my flat wearing a jersey and no shirt'. So, when M and J turned their back for a second, I grabbed Louise, already in her coat, and pushed her back into the drawing-room. They looked amazed at her disappearance but said nothing, and must have twigged; so I suspect I am now two friends the fewer. Another cloud was cast over the evening by the Old Dear, who had already protested at the party's being held at a weekend and thus preventing me from going to Frogs Cottage. She is now semi-officially at war with Ellénore and regards weekends as the principal theatre of operations: whoever gets me for Saturday and Sunday has won a battle. She arrived in a foul mood, having been unable to make the lift or the lights on the landing work. E, alarmed at the OD's breathlessness, asked her if she was all right, and had her head bitten off. 'I'm perfectly capable of walking up a few flights of stairs!' the OD snapped, and was frosty to E throughout the party despite the fact that the latter gave her a glass of Glenfiddich on the quiet. The venom-level soared as the OD was putting on her coat to leave and asked me whether I would be coming with her to the country next weekend as she wanted me to help her pick up the Elsan for Edie on the way. 'I'm afraid I can't come next weekend either,' I simpered. 'Right!' the OD spat through her teeth, 'I'm going to sell the house,' and flounced out of the door. Like most mothers, she half wants her son to have his own life and half wants him to remain a dependent three-year-old.

Addendum to the last instalment's reminiscences of temporary employment: Abram used to do similar jobs and once worked in the British Rail pensions department, where his job was to send standard letters to recently-bereaved widows of employees. Those of white-collar workers received a proper letter of condolence, while the relicts of engine drivers and the like were merely sent a form with name, pension and cause of death added by Abram's hand from a list. In the case of one recently deceased guard, A was struck to find that the cause of death, according to the list, was terminal incompetence. In fact the man had died of renal incompetence.

30 January

The smog of acrimony at the Empire Road Hermitage is now suffocatingly thick. I may have mentioned that Rackman, driven to distraction by Jow-enn's nocturnal visits to the lavatory, resolved to evict her. The poor woman was made so anxious by his complaints that she wanted to pee all the more, and a vicious circle was created, which I was sucked into one night. Walking up with a full bladder, I was frightened that R might burst out and strangle me as I creaked past his door, so I peed into the sink of the disused kitchen by my room. I had forgotten that the taps did not work, so I had to wash down the drips with my night-time glass of water. On other occasions I have braved the trip to the john but, while passing R's room, have walked with little steps, so that he would think I was Jow-enn. Cupidity got the better of Rackman and he decided not only to put up with Jojo but to take in a third lodger whom Stella had recommended – a female Scottish dancer. I was unable to discover whether she was a muckleflugging expert or just a dancer who happened to be Scottish, as she failed to turn up to inspect the premises. With luck, that is the last we shall hear of additional lodgers. Having decided to keep Jow-enn, Rackman realized that he might as well be civil to her, and to her amazement he started making merry conversation and even gave her roses on her birthday. This cheerful interval was brought to an abrupt close yesterday morning by an incident involving a toothbrush. J had locked herself in the bathroom for her usual four-hour lustration, and R wanted to brush his teeth. When he called frostily through the door, she would neither let him in nor pass the brush out, saying that she was washing her hair. Rackman, his voice quavering with fury, squeaked that he had a train to catch (they run every five minutes at that time) and that she had two minutes to give him his brush, and stormed back to his room. In the evening, unfortunately, we were all in the kitchen simultaneously, I eating steak, Rackman devouring fried lights with some pieces of sliced bread stirred in, and Jow-enn having her usual plate of Marks and Spencer coleslaw, royal jelly and a refreshing cup of hot water. R was still livid with J, and brooded over his

173

offal, refusing to speak. I gave up trying to make conversation and started filling in a Covent Garden booking form, while J pretended to read the *Catford Echo*. Eventually she decided that the barometer had fallen low enough and bravely started chatting to me, whereupon Rackman stalked from the room. It is unjust that I am fond of Rackman and can't stand Jojo. The main source of irritation is that she is so highly strung that another quarter-tone would snap the strings; the other night, she was near to tears because a taxi driver told her she was being too serious, studying classical music. It is also hard to put up with her bottomless ignorance; her not having heard of the *Critique of Pure Reason* is just forgivable, but it is an outrage that a pianist should not know that Beethoven's sonata op. III has only two movements.

When I had finished the New Year exams, I began to fantasize about having done brilliantly, and then began to half-believe the fantasy, smiling at the teachers with the star pupil's grin of complicity. This was a mistake. My confidence about the criminal paper was unfounded: I passed without many marks to spare, having overlooked the possibility of doing a man called Derek, in a question on rape, for indecent assault. In the two other papers that have so far been returned my marks have been merely respectable, and I have still to get back the paper on land law, in which I knew at the time that I was writing bilge. It would be less galling if some intellectual pygmies had not done better than I; a dopey creature called Sharon, who sucks sweets, talks about makeup and goes to discos, beat me in trusts. Worst of all, Barbara has done excellently throughout, and has made sure that we all know it. Last term she proclaimed haughtily that she never reveals her marks, but it turns out this means only that she doesn't reveal *bad* marks. She already (in the Old Dear's metaphysically puzzling phrase) 'thinks she's everybody', and will now be unbearable. I have no excuse for lack of brillance, having worked fairly hard and knowing the stuff fairly well. Seeing some question marks in red ink by some pellucid sentences in my contract paper, I thought of blaming the mediocre marks on illegible handwriting, but have decided to resign myself to the fact that I am thick. I joined a group of equally undistinguished candidates in the canteen, and we agreed that we were never all that interested in law anyway. 'I still see myself as a scientist,' said Dr Fisher, the former expert on cancer.

Explanation of two idioms: (1) When the Old Dear has run out of air freshener, she gets rid of smells by lighting a match. She claims this is the origin of the expression 'Cor, strike a light'. (2) The genitalia of the female skate are said to be like those of the female human, and it is alleged that fishermen resort to them during long trawls. When I mentioned this to Abram, he said he now knew what was meant by 'Get your skates on'.

6 February

Rackman has a papier-mâché pig called Darren, which is three feet long, two feet high and bright red, with a piece of string for a tail, to which is tied a pale blue bow of tulle. Strictly speaking, Darren is a piggybank, but his huge volume contains only one 2p coin, which Abram generously inserted after a lavish dinner. Darren usually lives under the rubber plant in the dining-room, from where he gazes at the three marquetry ducks flying up the opposite wall, but recently Rackman has started moving him about and one is occasionally startled by a snout poking unexpectedly round a door. The wee piggy has now been enlisted in his master's campaign against Jow-enn. With a view to terrifying her out of nocturnal micturition, Rackman, before turning in, sat Darren on the lavatory seat; but on the night in question Jojo's bladder remained empty and it was I, the following morning, who was given the fright. In revenge, after R had left for the office, I tucked Darren up in his bed. R has been unable to make me tell him whether I or Jow-enn did this, and says that if he knew it was J she would rise in his estimation. He cannot, of course, find out from her, as they are not on speaking terms, but seems to think I am the more likely farceur, as today I found Darren in my wardrobe, wearing my trilby hat. Rackman's instigation of this prep school merriment is explained by a rush of high spirits following the results of his ultrasound bath. The Indian doctor could find nothing wrong with R's testicles and could only suggest that the pain was caused by pressure from his vast belly. The doc also announced that Rackman was exceptionally fertile, his spermatozoa being sixty per cent active, thirty per cent sluggish and ten per cent non-motile.

Lectures at the Institute are depressing at the moment, tort in particular having taken a turn for the even nastier. This week we were told the damages to be expected for negligently caused loss of various parts of the body: £50,000 for an arm, £60,000 for a leg, £5,000 for a finger, £6,000 for a thumb, but not more than £100,000 for total paralysis. Mr Hackett observed that, if you are going to lose a limb, you should try to do so while you are in the USA, where damages run into millions. I still think £5,000 is not bad for a finger, and shall contrive to lose one if my grant runs out. There was also some cheery information about accidents turning people into vegetables. If the victim is in a coma, he cannot claim for pain and suffering, though he can recover for lost amenity; thus his relations will suddenly discover that he was a passionate footballer, in the hope of securing some dough for all the matches he is missing while lying in hospital with a tube up his nose. But you can't claim for lost amenity if you're dead, Hackett asserted wisely. A lecture on the Animals Act was enlivened by a case called *Behrens v Bertram Mills Circus*, the facts of which were these. A ringmaster, contrary to circus rules, had brought his small dog with him into the ring. While the elephants were doing their turn, the dog became excited and started yapping at them. The elephants, who were following each other in a circle round the ring, became nervous and started walking increasingly quickly, eventually breaking into a stampede, during which they trampled on a booth containing two midgets on display. The midgets, or their estates, were suing the circus. Another case – a variant of the bull in a china shop – involved an ox who ambled into an ironmongers and caused miscellaneous damage in the three hours it took to get him out. What is engaging about such cases is the animals' debonair disregard of the legal consequences of their actions.

I recklessly agreed to be a balloon-blowing skivvy for Augustus's fifth birthday party on Sunday afternoon. He shared the party with the son of the manager of the Porsche showroom (v. 13 December), so fifty infants were treated to sausages on sticks, jelly and Punch and Judy among the sports cars. I was overwhelmed by the occasion and fell on the neck of the Punch and Judy man when he muttered to me, 'I hate kids.' One or two fathers were present, who, to conceal their embarrassment, poured each other ostentatiously large whiskies and then huddled in corners from which they emitted bursts of false and raucous laughter while their wives rushed about the room trying to combine the roles of waitress and sergeant-major. One of the men, a braying buffoon with brylcreemed hair plastered over his bald patch, deigned briefly to participate by throwing paper plates in the air and was marched from the room by Ellénore. When the little mites, having stuffed themselves, started to become restless, I rushed for my coat and slunk off to the Empire Road Ivory Tower, to find that my bedroom ceiling had collapsed. I threatened Rackman with the Occupier's Liability Act 1957 and that night slept with my head under the pillow in fear of another Aberfan.

*

14 February

When Abram invites himself to Frogs Cottage for the weekend, he refuses to come on Friday evening in the car with the OD and me, and I am forced to meet him off a train the following morning. He almost always misses the train he has announced he will be on, so I wait, before driving to Dunham station, until the train has left London, so that I am still at home to receive his apologetic admission that he will be arriving an hour later. In pre-Samantha days he once invited himself and – to the fury of the OD, who muttered that she didn't see why she should entertain Abram's 'fancy ladies' – a gigantic American girl called Betsy. Their train was to leave Liverpool Street at 11.30 a.m. so, having at 11.40 answered the phone to hear the customary peep-peep-peep followed by some perfunctory grovelling, I set off to meet the 12.30, leaving the lunch to increase in carbon-content. The train arrived, the passengers alighted and dispersed, leaving me alone on the platform with a lunatic who sat singing to a ukulele. Abram and the giant were not to be seen. A porter then announced that, if there was a Mr North on the platform, he should drive eight miles down the line to a halt where his guests had got off in error. The train did not officially stop there, and had only paused at a signal, but Abram had dreamily led the human skyscraper on to the deserted platform, and it was only as the signal changed and the train pulled away that he noticed an unfamiliar level crossing and the absence of the familiar footbridge. I found the happy couple sitting among some levers in the crossing keeper's box, sheltering from the wind. Once I had stopped shrieking, I agreed with Abram, by means of nudges and winks, that it would be entertaining to convince the giant that I was a great landowner with a seat like Castle Howard, and we spent some time describing the grounds, the stables and the ancient family rituals in which she would be obliged to participate. As we approached Goose End, Abram said that on the way up to the manor we would be looking in on a little old lady who had faithfully served the family for many years and now lived in a charming white house called Frogs Cottage. It is a tribute to American egalitarianism that Betsy's manner towards the OD did not change when she realized the deception.

Last Saturday Abram came alone, having announced that he would like a weekend of fresh air (as usual he spent the whole time smoking by the fire), and on the Thursday evening he rang the OD to check 'that the invitation was still open'. 'I thought you had invited yourself,' she just managed to stop herself from saying. The OD finds Abram at least as irritating as I do. Usually she is enraged by the fact that he appears for breakfast when it is nearly lunchtime, but last Sunday he got into trouble by surfacing before she had made the toast. 'Go for a walk till I tell you to come in,' she snapped, so poor Abram went and shuffled round the lawn. 'Abram's a wally,' the OD complained later, 'he walked on the lawn when it was covered in frost.' She went on to describe him as 'a big baby' on the grounds that he never did anything for himself. The OD dislikes almost all my friends, and when one of them comes to stay she vents her spite on her son. On this occasion the outburst took the form of a harangue over dinner, to the effect that my learning Latin was part of a policy to put as great an intellectual distance between myself and other people as possible with a view to sneering at them. I almost proved her point for her by mounting the usual rejoinder that, life being so short, it is better to spend one's leisure pursuing the hard gemlike flame than nodding off over the middlebrow trash she skims through in bed while half-listening to radio phone-ins. 'Since we only have seventy-odd years on this planet . . .' I began portentously, choosing the number with care, '. . . we might as well spend them sitting about reading Latin!' interjected Abram, who then fell about with mirth. When

I glared at him, he cleared his throat and continued, 'Actually, I think it's admirable to teach yourself Latin.' 'Why don't you do it, then?' the OD barked, and I then unkindly rounded on my ally by reminding him that he gave up Greek lessons because he found the alphabet beyond him. The atmosphere cleared a little after the pudding, when I found the crackers we had forgotten to pull at Christmas, one of which contained the following riddle, 'Who wrote Great Eggspectations? Answer, Charles Chickens.' Underneath, the joke was attributed to one Brian Gobb of Help the Aged. Abram was then moved, as we washed up in paper hats, to recite an incomprehensible Jewish joke: one Jewish tailor says to another, 'My son has gone to grow oranges in Israel.' 'Ah,' the other replies, 'all one colour!'

During the interval of a concert at the Barbican on Friday, Mary told me of an old lady who taught her the violin and who, to disguise her wrinkles, used to wear strips of sellotape on her face – a remedy as outlandish as that of the waiter at Wheeler's in Old Compton Street who sought to disguise his bald patch by drawing black lines on his head in crayon. Mary also mentioned Hamish's latest request for items from his secret cupboard: the next parcel is to contain a wah-wah pedal, some special seaweed from Brittany, a Biggles scarf, a statue of Bhodidarma and some fish-oil tablets which, to prevent them from rattling, she is going to wrap in a Guatemalan cushion-cover.

22 February

Mary came to dinner on Wednesday, having spent the day in evening dress with the orchestra, posing for photographs. These were not for the orchestra's publicity but for an advertisement for a surgical appliance to prevent incontinence. Planted among the musicians was an actor pretending to be a cellist, who was photographed leaping from his seat in mid-symphony with a terror-stricken expression as he supposedly realized that he was about to soil himself. I remarked that it seemed an extravagance to hire a major orchestra for such a pic, but Mary explained that it was cheaper than using extras since the musicians already had the proper attire.

I am decreasingly honoured by my membership of the swot group at NIPLES, as discussion of legal questions is being replaced by gossip. At our last meeting most of the time was devoted to a spiteful dissection of an amiably oafish classmate called Dennis, whom the lesbian members of the group – Glenda and, it now emerges, Barbara – condemned chiefly on the ground that he exhibits certain characteristics typical of men. As I climbed under the table, Barbara reassured me that I did not have these traits and that I had only been elected to the group because the members felt sure they could treat me as an honorary woman. My relationship with Shirley has been soured by a contretemps at a tutorial. She announced to Mr Bennett, in a shop steward's manner, that we all felt he set too many questions. I neither felt this nor had been asked whether I did before S presumed to speak on my behalf, so – reflecting that, if I was no good at law, I had better rely on being teacher's pet – I said that I found the number of questions quite manageable. 'Thank you very much for your solidarity!' Shirley remonstrated after Bennett had left, and went on to announce, to my relief, that that was the last time she was going to speak up for the class. She appeared to have forgiven me by the afternoon, as she passed me a chocolate egg in the library. I am also disappointed by Annabel, the most winsome member of the swot group (faint praise), who lives in a hostel run by nuns. She became excited in a lecture on constitutional law, when she found on the list of cases a reference to Stevenage magistrates' court: she

181

nudged me, then pointed to the word 'Stevenage', then tapped herself on the chest, nodding and smiling. After the lecture she explained that this charade had meant that she came from Stevenage. 'How remarkable,' I managed to bleat. I am disheartened with the law, perhaps because I have not proved the juristic genius I had assumed I would be, and am plagued by the question whether I have made the wrong career decision.

I depressed myself with this topic, lying on the bed in Jeremy Hawthorn's Welsh cottage, where I had invited myself and Ellénore for the weekend. Jeremy, the Ben Gunn of Llandwynant, was pathetically grateful for the invitation, having managed to fill only a couple of pages in his visitors' book after six years. He painted a distressing picture of his life, with its solitary four-hour drives to Manchester nightclubs in the hope of meeting a girl. For some years he has been led a dance by a receptionist called Caroline, who, even by Jeremy's account, sounds a fiend. Rackman, a misogynist in any case, took a dislike to her when he gave her a lift from the cottage to London one weekend. For reasons I have been unable to establish, she was dressed in a nightie for the journey. She was also dehydrated, having kept Jeremy company in poculis the night before, and begged Rackman to stop at a motorway service station so she could have a drink. But Rackman, by now in the grip of a terrible hatred, refused to stop the car, and Caroline was forced to stick her head out of the window and open her mouth to catch raindrops. Later in the journey she wanted a cigarette, but Rackman, who was smoking himself, told her that he would not allow smoking in his car. Ellénore offered to introduce Jeremy to one of her girlfriends, but J turned out to want a partner of about half the average age of the Kensington coterie, so she then proposed fixing him up with her babysitter, a vigorous eighteen-year-old. E and I took a lot of exercise in bed, while Jeremy played Dichterliebe loudly on the gramophone, the walls of the cottage being thin. Our only outing was to the local town to fill his empty larder and fridge from a grim semi-supermarket, which was formerly called Nigel's Superstore but whose sign, with the passing of time, has come to read 'Nigl's Supersore'. It emerged that rural Wales has less in common with Ambridge than with Stalinist Russia: as we ate a sandwich in the pub and E and I asked Jeremy about local life, he became purple and, looking nervously round the room, would answer every question with 'I'll tell you later' muttered through the teeth. His uneasiness turned to panic when an elderly and burly man called Llewellyn tapped him on the shoulder. Llewellyn squatted beside Jeremy, whispered in his ear, then offered to buy us all drinks and then said mysteriously that he hoped Jeremy would shoot him before long. Jeremy was too shaken to tell us later what power Llewellyn had over him; all we could divine was that Ll was a family retainer of some kind. J is anxious to be on friendly terms with the townspeople and almost cried with embarrassment when one of the locals glared at me for unthinkingly murmuring 'What a language!' while looking at a poster in Welsh. He also pleaded with me to stop imitating the sepulchral Welsh 'O-o-o-o-oh' and commenting in public on Welsh people's curious use of 'Isn't it?', which they insert in syntactically inappropriate places, for example, 'O-o-o-o-oh, you'll have to keep the sheep out, isn't it, Jeremy?'

Envoi

Some readers foolishly expect diaries to end with a
bang, as if (a) the diarist's life could be relied on to reach
a climacteric on the day he decided to stop writing, or
(b) he should continue writing until something astonishing
happened, or (c) he should lapse at the end into fiction.
All I am prepared to offer – in the manner of an Xmas
letter from a tiresome American aunt you have not seen
for years – is an outline of events in the ten months
since my last entry, in the hope that temporal distance
will lend to the foregoing stuff the same unity as a
denouement would.

First, the Old Dear has decided to sell Frogs Cottage. It
has become more of a millstone than an idyll since the
84-year-old gardener fell forward on to the wheelbarrow, cracked his breastbone and left us to weed for
ourselves. Moreover the house has become infested
with rats. In the course of one week they gnawed
through three quarters of a structurally indispensable
beam, leaving a Matterhorn of chippings and plaster. It
would have been neater for the OD to wait until Edie
was, as Edie herself puts it, 'kicking up the daisies', but
Edie, though she now has the mental life of a stone,
grows plumper and rosier by the minute, as a result of
being cosseted by a series of live-in keepers. These
ladies, supplied by an agency called Caring Cousins,
stay for about a fortnight each and vary in degrees of
incompetence and eccentricity. There has been a fey

poetess, a bluff and multiple-chinned psychiatric nurse, who called me Moosh, and a woman of about fifty named Olive who told us that, when she called on Mr Bird, he sat down by her on the sofa and put his arm round her. It is alarming to think – and another good reason to sell – that Bird's amiable rustic façade has all these years concealed a sink of lechery. As Olive, like the Old Dear, comes from Birkenhead, the two became chums, and the former showed the latter the confidential reports that Edie's Caring Cousins write for their employer. One keeper, a neurotic woman called Wendy Windowes to whom the OD took an instant and requited dislike, had written, 'Edie detests Lady North. I [WW] call her [Lady N] "Dame Edna".' Lady North is consulting her solicitor. The keepers seek to occupy Edie by giving her jigsaws, the sensible ones providing brightly coloured puzzles with two pieces, but the other day the Old Dear found Edie sitting vacantly in front of a 1000-piece Mappa Mundi in shades of grey. 'I must have a holiday,' Edie confided to her despairingly, 'they make me do these things, and it's awfully hard work.' Edie then looked out of the window and saw me mowing her lawn. 'That's my son,' she said. 'No he isn't, he's mine!' retorted the OD. 'Oh he is, you know, I've had him for years,' Edie replied with a dreamy smile. Some of the Caring Cousins are robust enough to stay with E repeatedly, but most refuse to go near the place again, so the agency finds it increasingly hard to service her. In cases of acute staff shortage a family of yobbos from Knatworth is called in, who turn poor Edie's bungalow into a scene from No Man's Land. While one of them, a thug with a crewcut and tattoos, was standing guard, Edie's cleaning lady found a bottle of green liquid and asked him what it was. 'We give it to her when she's naughty,' he said in a leaden voice. Unwisely the yobbos left the liquid behind when they moved out, and the cleaner took it to the doctor for analysis. It turned out to be a liquid cosh which, the doctor said, it is an offence to administer without prescription.

I left Ellénore in August, after a purgatorial week in her holiday flat in a Spanish condominium, where she discussed recipes with her girlfriend Dorabella while their children squabbled and gawped at pop videos. There was little to do but sit on the beach listening to other people's radios; reading was impossible and sunbathing a bore, so I sat scowling and pallid under a parasol while German youths playing football kicked sand into my eyes. As Ellénore drove me to the airport for my flight home, we arranged that I would come for supper on the night of her return some weeks later. I resolved that that supper should be our last, and in the meantime wrote to Ellénore to prepare her for what I intended to be an amicable farewell. The letter was meant to be jovially polemical, but my pen ran away with me and I ended up writing that she was intellectually vacant, that her affections were indiscriminate and that her social life was a comedy of manners comprising hen parties and genteel dinners. Unsurprisingly, when I turned up, I received a welcome as cool as the Pleistocene Epoch, and we parted with some acrimony. I had feared that I would feel lonely after the break, but found myself rejoicing at liberty regained. We were hopelessly ill-assorted: what should have been a romp of a few weeks ended a year too late. In the course of the autumn I have resumed relations with the cruelly abused Miss Bochvar, to whom I have proposed marriage. A woman with more magnanimity than sense, she has said she will think about it.

By doing violence to my brain, I managed to pass my first-year exam at NIPLES and am now embarked on a course that gives a new dimension to the concept of boredom. Last year the syllabus, dealing with general principles, was moderately entertaining; this year we are rewarded for parroting information I am ashamed to recite, such as that, to change the name of a private company limited by shares, a special resolution of members must be passed and a memorandum as amended, together with a fee of £40, sent to the Registrar of Companies within fifteen days. I had assumed that facts like this were the domain of sub-legal stooges, but it turns out that the stooge, *c'est moi*. The only subjects of any interest this year – and it is a sign of mental deterioration that I can find anything interesting in them – are revenue law and evidence. Revenue has the labyrinthine complexity of medieval theology; the lecturer will explain an opaque clause of the Finance Act by showing how it precludes some tax avoidance device that would never have entered my head in a thousand years, let alone during the few months such Acts remain in force. The *Vergänglichkeit* of fiscal legislation makes it hardly worthwhile to master it, and I have a new respect for Rackman – a specialist in tax – who must empty and refill his head with the stuff every April 6th. The chief attraction of evidence is the lecturer, Miss Tweedie, who is about my age and must be a colonel's daughter. She has wide eyes, a baby's smile and alabaster hands with delicate blue veins, wears stand-up collars and pearls, has a velvet band in her hair and talks in a canary-like voice with a whistly 's' about the most gruesome cases. 'The next example,' she warbled, a tiny muscle twitching in her neck, 'concerns a woman whose throat was sslit' – and went on to tell a hair-raising story about blood and semen.

I had resolved to be more friendly towards other students this academic year, but the resolution flagged on first inspection of my classmates. They are an even less prepossessing bunch than last year's: most have just have taken a law degree (such students are spared the NIPLES foundation course I took last year) and conseqently are ignorant of everything but the law.

Some are ignorant even of that. One specimen, a youth called Colin with blubber-lips, spotty cheeks, simian brow and grey shoes, is clearly mentally retarded but is nevertheless pleased with himself. Whenever a lecturer poses a question, rhetorical or otherwise, to the class, Colin will always blurt out an answer, and it will always be wrong. His friends have got wise to this and egg him on. The other day, in a conveyancing class, we were asked whether a certain clause amounted to a covenant or an easement. It was obviously a covenant, but Colin's neighbour whispered to him, 'It's an easement, isn't it, Colin?' 'Wuh, easement!' roared Colin, beaming at the rest of the class as they hid their faces in their hands. Colin even managed a shout of high-pitched laughter halfway through the end-of-term civil litigation exam. At the other end of the spectrum is a polite, pretty and modest girl called Sue with a huge legal brain. 'I wonder if we might circumvent the problem by securing a float-ing charge?' she suggested brilliantly, none of us knowing what a floating charge was. I am dismayed to find that she is going to Savage Borman, where she will be promoted to senior partner even more quickly than I am demoted to tea-lady. Her rise may however be checked by her pencilcase, which carries a picture from *Winnie the Pooh.*

I am so disheartened by the past fifteen months' cram-ming that I have been reduced to Hamishian vacillation by an unexpected opportunity to return to philosophy. One of the countless philosophical posts I applied for before turning to law was a teaching fellowship at my old college in Oxford. In the event, as a result of the usual lack of funds, the fellowship was suspended. But a fortnight ago my old director of studies, the Revd Howard Seed, rang to say that a four-year appointment is to be made next year and that, if I am prepared to be considered, I shall almost certainly be the lucky fellow. This proves that the old college tie is more potent than the strongest inductive evidence, for my career at Oxford was a catalogue of debauchery and my teachers despaired of me. On one occasion Seed invited me to his rooms for a pep talk and what he ludicrously called 'a jar of tay', but neither had any effect, as he is a buffoon, his own sole contribution to philosophy being a slim volume in a lurid purple cover with a title like *Torture, Suffering, Incest and Death*, on sale only in the college chapel. It is hard to know what to do. In favour of the job are the facts (i) that it will give me four relatively undisturbed years to work on the theory of rationality and (ii) that it is as good an opening as any to an academic career. Against it there are various considerations. In the first place, it is temporary and may result in my rejoining the philosophical superfluous men at an age when I am even less capable than now of learning new tricks. In the second, the pay is derisory, whereas the law can be a ladder to riches beyond the dreams of avarice. Neither of these points, if I take the job, will encourage Miss Bochvar to consent (I was recently struck by a sentence from an exercise in my Latin textbook, 'He was so poor that he was unattractive to women'). In the third place, while the NIPLES course is a test of endurance, I have heard that being a real solicitor is not so bad; and in any case, having adjusted my self-image to a legal career, I would find it a jolt reverting to a former self. And what would I say to Savage Borman, who have been paying my fees and maintenance? They stated that the money had no strings, but probity would oblige me to repay it, which would almost reduce my fellow's stipend to a negative figure. The $64k question is how much I want to do philosophy. As with many of the dissatisfied Socrateses I know, my education has infected me with the doctrine that the contemplative life is the only one worth living, but whether it is worth sacrificing so much to philosophy must depend in part on how good at philosophy I am. There are five grades of philosopher: the all-time greats, like Aristotle; the all-time second-rankers, like Schopenhauer; the men who are luminaries in their day but then forgotten, like uncle Jake; the journeymen; and the incompetents. I make the fourth grade and might one day make the third, but is it worth being a third-rate philosopher? I shall give it some thought.

A SELECTION OF FINE NOVELS
AVAILABLE FROM BLACK SWAN

☐	99075 2	QUEEN LUCIA	E.F. Benson	£4.99
☐	99076 0	LUCIA IN LONDON	E.F. Benson	£4.99
☐	99083 3	MISS MAPP	E.F. Benson	£3.99
☐	99084 1	MAPP AND LUCIA	E.F. Benson	£4.99
☐	99087 6	LUCIA'S PROGRESS	E.F. Benson	£4.99
☐	99088 4	TROUBLE FOR LUCIA	E.F. Benson	£3.99
☐	99202 X	LUCIA IN WARTIME	Tom Holt	£4.99
☐	99281 X	LUCIA TRIUMPHANT	Tom Holt	£4.99
☐	99348 4	SUCKING SHERBET LEMONS	Michael Carson	£4.99
☐	99340 9	ALL ABOUT ANTHRAX	Ross Fitzgerald	£3.99
☐	99338 7	PUSHED FROM THE WINGS	Ross Fitzgerald	£3.99
☐	99368 9	LOVE ON A BRANCH LINE	John Hadfield	£4.99
☐	99362 X	THE RUB OF THE GREEN	William Hallberg	£4.99
☐	99169 4	GOD KNOWS	Joseph Heller	£3.95
☐	99195 3	CATCH-22	Joseph Heller	£5.99
☐	99208 9	THE 158LB MARRIAGE	John Irving	£4.99
☐	99204 6	THE CIDER HOUSE RULES	John Irving	£5.99
☐	99209 7	THE HOTEL NEW HAMPSHIRE	John Irving	£4.99
☐	99369 7	A PRAYER FOR OWEN MEANY	John Irving	£5.99
☐	99206 2	SETTING FREE THE BEARS	John Irving	£4.99
☐	99207 0	THE WATER METHOD MAN	John Irving	£4.99
☐	99205 4	THE WORLD ACCORDING TO GARP	John Irving	£4.95
☐	99141 4	PEEPING TOM	Howard Jacobson	£3.95
☐	99063 9	COMING FROM BEHIND	Howard Jacobson	£3.99
☐	99252 6	REDBACK	Howard Jacobson	£4.99
☐	99351 4	BLUE HEAVEN	Joe Keenan	£4.99